Kalopsia

Kalopsia

Lucinda Lamont

Copyright (C) 2018 Lucinda Lamont
Layout design and Copyright (C) 2018 Creativia
Published 2018 by Creativia
Cover art by Cover Mint
This book is a work of fiction. Names, characters, places, and incidents are the product of the author's imagination or are used fictitiously. Any resemblance to actual events, locales, or persons, living or dead, is purely coincidental.
All rights reserved. No part of this book may be reproduced or transmitted in any form or by any means, electronic or mechanical, including photocopying, recording, or by any information storage and retrieval system, without the author's permission.

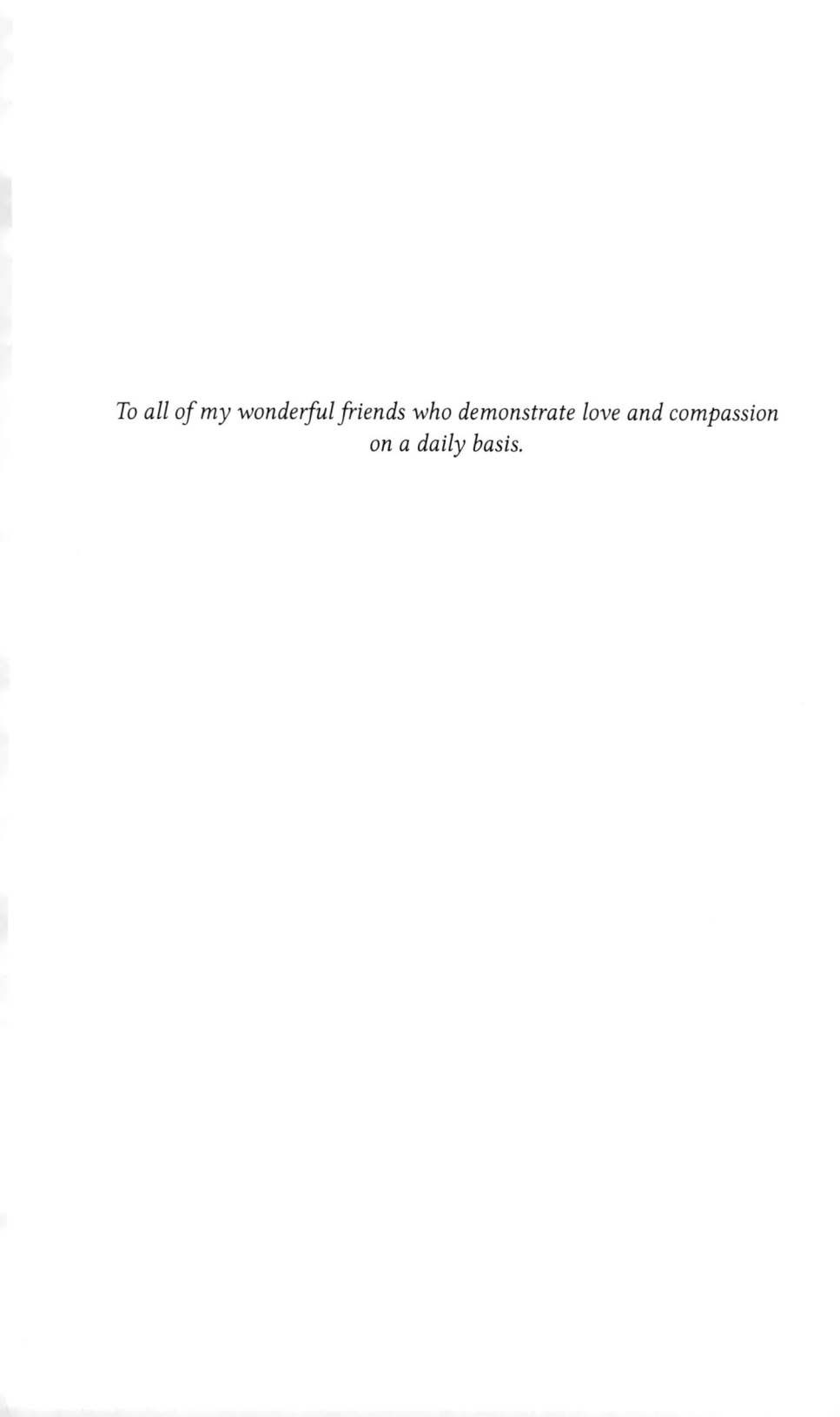

To all of my wonderful friends who demonstrate love and compassion on a daily basis.

Chapter 1

God I'm bored. How can I be bored, sipping on a large G&T, sitting outside a vibrant bar on La Rambla in Barcelona? Because, he's boring. I must do something about this. I'm not even happy on holiday anymore. Look at his stupid face. He doesn't even know I'm bored. We haven't spoken since we sat down and he doesn't even care. Maybe he likes to be quiet but I don't. I like to have fun, especially on holiday. If I was with my friends now we would all be struggling to get a word in edgeways and having a great time. But no, that doesn't happen with him. He enjoys being a moody bastard, at least it certainly seems that way. Oh well, at least I'm not at work. Although saying that, I have a laugh at work. My colleagues make me laugh but Tom doesn't. Tom doesn't know how to spell the word laugh let alone actually do it. The most excitement I've had today is this G&T. They've put a cinnamon stick in it which threw me a bit. As I watched the barman get out his jar of Gin accessories I thought, *steady on Pedro, cool your jets* but he assured me it was all the rage and to give credit where it's due, it works. Pedro knows his Gin alright. That excitement lasted about sixty seconds and now I'm sat here with Mr Miserable. Mr 'I can't let you out of my sight and I will never make you happy but if you leave me I will kill you' and I'm having an utterly shit time with the miserable, controlling prick.

Across the way there is another bar, well, La Rambla is crammed with bars from top to bottom. All of them heaving with bohemian residents and excitable tourists all wanting refreshment in the wonderful Mediterranean heat. Refreshments and big juicy olives and bread you can dip in oil and balsamic vinegar. Divine. There is a girl right in my eye line and she is laughing. *Bitch.* Look at her with her boyfriend/husband who makes her laugh heartily. She isn't even fake laughing like I do when he tells me one of his jokes that even a twelve-year old wouldn't find funny, but I detect his attempt at humour and offer the most lacklustre chuckle on autopilot. I wonder what he said to her to make her so happy? Maybe it wasn't even that funny, she just likes him. It's easier to find people funnier when you *actually* like them. Maybe it's her gay best friend. That's why she is in stitches because he's always funny. Not an arsehole most of the time but suddenly has a funny side when he has an audience. Yeah, I bet that's it.

We arrived in Barcelona two hours ago and already he was beginning to drink himself into oblivion. I haven't always hated him. There was a time when I was attracted to him, I think it was just before he revealed himself to be a complete wanker. We had a year of bliss, barely argued. He was charming, he tried with my friends and my family and always wanted to be with me. Everywhere I went, everything I did, he was there. Right by my side. The problem is I should've spotted that he was insecure, possessive and controlling but because the boyfriend before him couldn't care less whether he saw me once a week or once a month, I took Tom's behaviour as a good thing. I thought we were having a proper relationship and building a life together.

He has a kid. The last boyfriend had a moped. He has a serious job…and serious baggage. All of this I took, bizarrely, as a good thing. I thought it was the most grown up relationship I had ever had and that this is what people do. I was twenty five and he was thirty eight when we met. He was divorced and needy. I was getting broody and needy. Needy for a serious relationship. As I said, the first year was great. He swept me off my feet. He took me away on romantic weekends without warning – meaning I had to cancel plans I had made with friends because he had 'surprised' me. My friends didn't mind the first, second and some, the third time. By the fourth time they all hated him and could see what I couldn't. Even this weekend, here we are in Barcelona when we were supposed to be staying with my friends in London. He booked the trip this morning and I had to let my friend, Sam, down again. She went mental, told me he was a dick and slammed the phone down. Tom said she wasn't a nice friend and that I shouldn't waste my time with people like her. I knew she was right but I didn't want him punching the kitchen cupboard doors next to my face again if I challenged him so I put on a fake smile, reluctantly packed my weekend bag and told Sam we weren't coming – again. She was in the supermarket buying all the food and drink for the spread she was planning and she cried as she tried to juggle her two small children and her disappointment with me, who she had been so desperately looking forward to seeing apparently.

I don't know why half my friends talk to me anymore. The amount of invitations I have accepted but cancelled later or just simply failed to show. My friend Claire told me recently I am now on her 'invite but won't turn up' list. That made me feel sad. To be honest, I didn't realise my friends liked me as much as they did until I started pissing them off. Now I have realised as I am losing them all. I'm losing them all because of this prick sat next to me.

I have been desperate to escape for some time. Desperate to end this miserable relationship but the truth is, he scares me. He told me if it wasn't for his daughter, he would have his ex-wife killed. He said he knows people that would do it for him. I had been in an abusive relationship when I was seventeen. It ended with me in the back of an ambulance with a broken nose. I swore I would never end up in something like that again. But I have. In fact, I think this is worse. This one is mental abuse. That's the reason we clash so much because I won't bow down to him. He is a bully but he won't leave me. I wish he would. I have even thought about how I would pretend to be upset if he told me it was over. I couldn't show him how thrilled I was because he might have me murdered so I would have to pretend to be devastated. I think I could pull it off.

Women are very good when they want something. I'm pretty sure I could pull it off. *Please don't go Tom! Please! We can fix this. Don't break the dream, don't take it away! I am nothing without you. You complete me! I'll even let you paint me like one of your French girl's!* Then pose like Kate Winslet did in Titanic and gesture towards him to paint me. He would laugh at how desperate I was, thrilled that he had won but as soon as he left and the front door had closed I could pop open the bubbly and put on Katrina and The Waves – Walking on Sunshine, on my boom bar full blast. Loud enough for him to hear it as he got in his car outside and then he would look in to the window with a face full of venom and I would be dancing and laughing at him whilst giving him the two fingers with both hands. Ok, perhaps I am thinking about this too much.

'Do you want another one babe?'

Bloody hell, he's drinking quickly. I hate it when he calls me babe in his horrible mock cockney voice. I don't mind a cockney voice as it goes but his is more Joe Pasquale and basically, I just don't like anything about him anymore. I don't like his stupid voice or his stupid face.

'Yeah go on then. Why not. We are on holiday I suppose.'

I don't look at him. I just continue to people watch up and down La Rambla. God, I love it here. I love all the stalls which all sell exactly the same things. Fridge magnets, postcards, aprons, castanets, playing cards, keyrings and the like. I wonder how they all manage to survive when they are all selling the same stuff? These people inspire me. They are always jolly and they never stop trying to get the sale. They reach out to any passer-by that they can make eye contact with and ninety nine percent of the time not only do they not get the sale, they don't even get acknowledged. I always say, 'No thank you' and I give them a big smile. I doubt it helps but I just admire their tenacity.

I look around and see him sitting there smirking away to himself. Why does he always do that? Sitting there smirking, what's he got to be so happy about? Then I notice he is ogling a hen party at a bar opposite. The group of women are barely dressed and extremely inebriated. Just how he likes his women I suppose. Fingers crossed one of them is up for it, they can have him. I wish I was here on my own and then some hunk with a tanned and toned body which is dripping in oil (hey this is my fantasy, don't judge) would come and sit next to me and charm me with his Spanish and we would fall in love because he would be a bloody nice bloke and not a complete wanker.

'So babe, where do you want to eat tonight?'

'Well, there is a place in the Gothic Quarter that has top ratings on Trip Advisor. The chef is Irish apparently. I thought maybe we could check that out?'

'Gothic Quarter? I'm not going there. Won't it be full of freaks who are miserable and they all have black hair? Fuck that babe. Let's go to an Irish bar, the footy is on tonight.'

'What is the point in asking me then if you already knew what you wanted to do?'

'Don't start a row with me babe, we are on holiday. Why have you always got to fucking start a fight.'

'How have I started a row? You asked me a question?'

'Shut up, you silly cow, you are always looking for an argument.'

And, so it begins. We landed less than twelve hours ago and he has probably had twice the amount of drinks than we have had hours here. Welcome to another lovely trip away with this prick.

The evening went on and I managed to get by without an argument by simply keeping my mouth shut and massaging my darling spouse's ego. I laughed in the right places, faked interest in his stories and said that I would be delighted to go to the Irish bar and have chicken wings and watch the footy.

Did I want to go down near the water and find a nice Mediterranean bar serving up local cuisine? Nah! Did I want massive shrimps loaded with garlic and oil? No way José! Did I want a cocktail whilst listening to the water lapping the shore on the wonderful man-made beach of Barcelona? No Sir-ee! Please, let's travel to a foreign country and pile into a place that is full of British tourists, watching British sport and eating food that can be found in any dump back in Britain.

Anything that can be served as a feast or super-sized or gigantic is vulgar to me. I want enough food. I don't want a tiny portion that is only good for an Instagram photo. I want a normal portion. You shouldn't get a pat on the back for over indulging. It's nothing short of grotesque. When he finished his ridiculous amount of chicken wings and looked at me with orange sauce all around his mouth, I wanted to ask him how he managed to get out of his highchair, ask him where his bib was and start wiping his face. The fact that he was so pleased with himself made him look a bigger tool than normal. I managed to drift through the evening in a haze of spiced rum and ginger beer loveliness.

He was much more tolerable when I was wrapped up in the warm embrace of alcohol. That was the other problem. He is a big drinker and so I have become a big drinker. I am nowhere near on his level of dependency despite his best efforts. I nag him about his drinking because he does it every day and it's not just a beer. It starts off with about three beers and then he will open a bottle of wine and then he moves on to the shorts. Every. Day. I have tried telling him I don't want to drink everyday but I come in from work and he already has one poured on the side waiting for me. I guess we both win if I drink. I find him more bearable and as a result, I am probably nicer to him. He's like a drug dealer keeping me topped up on his opium, never letting me have a day off in case I get a taste of how good seeing and thinking straight could be. The more he keeps me boozed up, the more he can try and control me and our miserable life. What he doesn't realise is that he doesn't need to try that hard or spend that much. I'm too scared to leave him anyway, in case he kills me.

Chapter 2

I woke up next to him snoring this morning in his deep, boozy, Barcelona stupor. I deserve a medal for not elbow dropping him there and then as I crept out of bed and into the shower. On the way back from the bar last night, he tried getting all fruity with me and became quite forceful. He tried getting me to have sex with him in an alleyway, against a bin of all places. He was hammered. This is what he does. Treats me like crap all day and then pretends to be nice when he's drunk knowing full well that he will want sex by the end of the night. He thinks I can't see through him. He thinks he's clever. I think he's disgusting and I must start making a plan to get away from him.

After my refusal to have sex on a bin we broke out into an argument as we walked back to the hotel. He called me the usual. A boring bitch. A miserable cow. He said it's not right for me to refuse him and that he won't be happy unless we have sex that night. As we got back to our room I told him that we would not be having sex. I cried. He had been so horrible and aggressive. I explained that I didn't like it when he got this drunk and that it didn't make me want to have sex with him. He pushed me onto the bed. He told me to shut up. I pushed him off. He lay on top of me with his hand around my throat. He told me I was nothing but a frigid bitch and that he would find it somewhere else. He then left the room.

I didn't care. I was glad he left me alone. As I drifted off to sleep, I prayed that he would never return.

As the morning sidled in through the shutters I was disappointed to see my prayers hadn't been answered so I got up and showered. I knew what was coming next. He would be up soon and he would act like nothing happened. He would dismiss all of it. I wouldn't be reminding him either. When I have done that in the past, he only reacts badly and he scares me so I just roll with it. I accept it and carry on in this miserable existence, fantasising about my escape.

I was right. By the time I came out of the bathroom he had stirred. I got dressed in the bathroom because I can't bear him looking at me after a night like that. I don't want him anywhere near me. He tells me to make him a coffee and winks at me.

He's got a fucking cold sore. He went out last night to I don't know where and he has woken up with a fucking cold sore. What the hell has he been doing? Actually, I don't want to know. I gladly make him a coffee as it means I don't have to look at him. I know I said I wouldn't say anything but coming home with a virus on his face is a new low. I can't help but enquire.

'Where did you end up last night then?'

'Nowhere. I didn't go out.'

'You did. We fell out and you went out. You were cross with me.'

'I just went outside and had a cigarette to calm down. I was back in five minutes later and you were asleep.'

That's a lie, I clock watched for at least forty minutes.

'Oh right. Well, it's a new day. Let's forget about it and get out in the glorious sunshine.'

I smiled at him and gave him his coffee.

'Is that my apology? You really are a piece of fucking work, Kate. You're lucky I am so reasonable.'

'Sorry Tom. Sorry about last night.'

'Whatever.'

My stomach is churning with anxiety and stress. For the last twelve month's I have had crippling stomach pains and fatigue because of the monster that I live with. I can't tell him I don't feel well. This won't surprise you but sympathy isn't a strong point of his either.

About twenty minutes later we are both ready to leave the hotel and head out for breakfast. I feel happier now because I am safer outside. He can't scare me or be nasty to me when we are out. He likes everyone to think he is the nicest guy out there so I will now get at least eight hours of pleasantries. It pisses me off that this is how he is but the outdoor version is easier to handle than the at home version.

It's funny isn't it, yesterday I was dreading the drinking pattern starting and yet today I can't wait to down my first, oversized, fish bowl of Gin and Tonic. The stronger the better. If I drink it quickly it will make me feel numb for a while.

We are staying just a short distance from La Rambla. A few metro stops to be precise but the weather is gorgeous and so we decide to stroll and see what's around. He seems happy, he definitely had sex last night. It's so obvious when his balls have been emptied. I don't care. It saved me a job and has made today more relaxed.

When I am in Europe I love to just walk around the streets and take it all in. The air smells different. The heat feels different. The hustle and bustle is different. We were out just before the shops and cafés began to open so we saw bakery drivers and the like all delivering their goods to the various establishments. Even the drivers seem happier than British drivers. Is it the sun? Is it the heat? Is it just Spain? Or maybe they all just got laid last night.

As we stroll, I almost creak my neck looking up at all the tall apartment buildings. I picture myself opening my shutter doors and putting washing out to dry before heading down to La Sagrada Familia to meet friends for a coffee. I imagine that I would be so happy living here that I would be skipping my way down the street. Whilst I ponder that for a moment we notice that a market is being set up and coming to life as well. There is so much going on. Numerous food stalls, craft stalls, books, clothes, music. I check my watch and it's just before 8.30am. Before I know it some sort of Spanish marching band appear playing music and everyone stops to let them cross the street and continue with their parade. It seems like something just out of a movie and it makes me love the place even more. How wonderful it must be to look out to this every weekend from your apartment window. That's it, I've decided. If Tom and I split, I am moving to Barcelona.

We find a quaint little café and order some breakfast and sit outside. This is the life. Glorious sun and a vibrant community. What a great way to spend a Saturday morning. My bowl of fresh fruit and yogurt are brought out along with my fresh orange juice and black coffee. I had wanted a cheese and ham toastie this morning. I fancied the grease to soak up last night's booze but Tom ordered without asking me and seeing as we were off to a good start I didn't want to rock the boat.

We sit and eat in silence. I don't mind the peace at this time of day. It can take me a while to come around in the mornings so I am glad that we aren't talking. I am just looking around, taking it all in and people watching. I love looking at all the architecture. Gaudi's work is incredible. We are sitting not far from La Sagrada Familia and I watch the flock of tourists milling about already forming a long queue to get inside. There's no doubt about Gaudi's talent but I can't understand why he went to so much trouble to make the spires look like they were melting. Maybe it's because he had been drawing his plans for so long and in the end, he thought he couldn't be arsed and so he just drew some squiggly lines. Maybe he thought he would come back to that bit later but he died before he could and now the builders are trying to build something he didn't intend to look like that. I like that idea. I chuckle to myself.

'What's funny babe?'
'Oh, nothing really.'
'Come on, tell me.'
'I was just imagining Gaudi giving up with his drawings and that's why a lot of that building looks like it's melting.'
'What?'
'Don't worry.'
'What the fuck are you talking about?'
'The Cathedral. There. That fuck off massive building that is swamped with tourists, mainly Chinese. The guy that designed it was called Gaudi.'

'Really? How do you know so much about it?'

'I looked up things to see and do before we came.'

'See and do? We know what we want to see and do. We want to sit in the sun and drink. I think it's sweet when you try to be clever. You're not fooling me babe.'

We both picked up our coffee and took sips in silence.

The rest of the day went by kind of painlessly. We mooched about in the heat whilst stopping off at an array of bars for refreshments. He was happy and so, I was happy. We had lunch down by the marina overlooking the fabulous yachts they have moored up. Many of the yachts had British flags on them and one of them which looked particularly grand had a guy running on his treadmill on the third deck. What a life. Not bad for some. That's something to aspire to. Make millions of pounds, move to Barcelona, get a three or four tier yacht and have a treadmill in one of the rooms that you can use whilst looking out over the bay. What a lucky bastard. I wonder if he's single? Even if he is, he won't be looking for a twenty something, slim blonde with a psycho ex in tow.

We spent the afternoon continuing to walk and stroll and drink and eat. The life of Barcelona was seeping into my skin. I was falling in love with the place more and more.

We went back to our hotel to freshen up for the evening. As we went into our room it was clear Tom had only one thing on his mind and I couldn't think of a reason to say no. I mean, the fact I didn't want to was surely good enough but not if I wanted to be able to enjoy the rest of our weekend here and so I allowed him. He lowered his slightly overweight body on to mine. All I could smell was smoke and beer on him and he stank. His technique wasn't great either. He thought he was great.

Well he would say he thought he was great but the fact he insisted on having the lights off said otherwise. It used to annoy me when we first started out, now I thought it was a blessing. I knew that I must do something about us soon. Him being on me made me feel sick. My body would recoil and I would silently beg for it to be over as quickly as possible. These days his best was about two minutes but for me it seemed like two hours. I hated pretending to connect and be involved and the only sense of euphoria I experienced was when he got off.

I went to the shower and I cried. He was sleeping as he so often did straight after. Two minutes really took it out of him so it would seem.

I'm not naturally a quiet crier so to sob in the shower took great skill to try and do so discreetly. I didn't want him to know something was up. I couldn't talk to him about it. What could I tell him? *You scare the shit out of me and I'm scared you are going to kill me and that's why I stay.* I hate confrontation. It's not a conversation I can have and that's why I cry in the shower when he's not around. I am stuck between the 'run for your life or put up and make do' scenario.

Not many of my relationships have been great. What if I leave him just to walk into another disaster? At least being with him, I know the dangers. If he kills me then so be it. My time will be up and there is nothing I will be able to do about it. If I leave him I would always be looking over my shoulder.

Chapter 3

We boarded the plane to come home and I was delighted to see that a woman who thought more of herself than she should had the pleasure of sitting next to my vile boyfriend. I knew this would please him and it pleased me. I could sleep and relax knowing that he had everything he needed around him. Drinks on tap, a desperate bimbo sitting next to him and me not going anywhere. As I drifted off to sleep with my head leaning uncomfortably against the plastic window (*can they not cushion the walls on these things?*) I could hear her telling him that he wouldn't believe how white her white bits were. They seemed like the perfect couple. Hopefully he would leave me for her. They could swap numbers whilst I was asleep and meet up when we got back.

As I played out that thought in my head I felt a pang of pain in my stomach as memories of his cheating came back to me. Cheating he always denied but how many "ex-girlfriends could there be that hadn't gotten over him" as he alleges?

He has treated me like such a fool and I have let him crawl back time and time again. Would his phone go off through the night for the rest of our days to come? Would I catch him looking at dating websites again "because he thought he saw someone he knew on his old account that he doesn't know how to close?" How many more times would he come back with foundation on his shirt and glitter on his cheek? Or what about the time I left something at home and caught him in the shower at 11am after he had one at 8am? And not forgetting the time I was rushed into hospital with a particularly nasty virus and I couldn't get hold of him. It later turned out he was "catching up with an old friend" and was not able to answer his phone. Cock.

The last couple of days of our painstakingly long weekend passed with me playing ball and trying to do the impossible, keep Tom happy. We did the same every day. Walked around, popped in and out of shops, stopped for drinks and snacks, back to the hotel for tedious sex and then back out for the evening so he could get shitfaced and we could pretend to be happy. I couldn't wait to get home and get back to work.

How I avoided my first proper smack from him last night was strange though. We were sitting outside of the last bar, having a night cap as he calls it. I had had far too much to drink and the truth had started to come out. We were bickering. He told me how lucky I was and how I would never find someone like him again. No one else would put up with my shit apparently. I let him ramble as I struggled to keep my eyes open, I was desperate for my head to hit the pillow but we still had a ten-minute walk to get back to the hotel and I was flagging. I finally bit when he told me that above all else, no one could satisfy me like he did. I choked on my drink and sprayed it everywhere as I began to laugh which obviously infuriated him. He asked what I thought was so funny and demanded that I tell him. The moment was almost sobering but, not quite. For the first time in over a year, I found some guts or maybe it was stupidity masquerading as guts. I put my glass down on the table and looked him square in the eye.

'You are not the best I've ever had. Far from it. The best I have ever had was Jamie. He was huge and he could go for hours. Your penis is barely a penis. It's like a penis gave birth to a baby penis. I didn't care when I liked you, my love for you superseded your goldfish like penis! So no, you're not the best or anywhere near the biggest.'

I delivered it slowly and with conviction. I didn't blink and my face told him he disgusted me. What happened next, I was not expecting.

He said nothing. He stood up. Picked up his beer and downed it.

'Come on. It's time for bed.'

I stood up. Left my drink and we walked back. Silently.

He got into bed and he went to sleep. Not a peep out of him. I just hoped I would wake up in the morning.

I did wake up, clearly, as I'm now on the plane home and no more has been said. Not a word. I wonder if he can't remember. Of course, he remembers! He doesn't forget anything. No amount of alcohol effects his memory which is surprising.

He is probably planning my death. He knows I have to come home from Barcelona. He knows my friends are expecting me. He's probably making a mental shopping list of what to buy to get rid of me:

Rope, bin bags, chain saw (?), acid (?), elephant tape, shovel. Who knows how he will do it but he must be thinking about it. He wants his ex-wife dead for whatever reason and last night I told him he's shit in bed with a small willy so my cards are definitely marked.

I awoke with a thud, literally. We had just landed. I must've fallen asleep before take - off. That pleases me. Two hours of my life not wasted with him I guess. He is hammered. Him and his new bimbo mate are trolleyed. I see them swap numbers as I stir. They didn't see me wake. Mind you, they probably can't see anything in their state. I animatedly stretch and rub my eyes. He puts his hand on my knee whilst not taking his eyes off her and they are giggling away about something. I don't know, I don't care. I stand up and they try to do the same but both fall back into their seats and begin to laugh hysterically.

They are the only ones laughing. She is mixed race with a fantastic afro hairdo and at one time was probably quite attractive. She is wearing a long black maxi dress and as she is leaning forward, seemingly in hysterics, you can see straight down this dress of hers which reveals her tits. Both of them. Nipples and all. She's had a few kids. Either that or she was in an African tribe where she had to carry twenty paving slabs daily which were secured through nipple piercings in her now seemingly empty breasts. She's probably a nice lady. I shouldn't be a bitch. Actually, no. Even though he is an arse, he is clearly my arse and she knows it. So, that makes her a bitch. It can't have been twenty paving slabs, I'm upping it to forty.

The plane begins to empty and I am left to get our carry-on luggage whilst he exits with his new friend. I struggle collecting our two small cases and his three duty free bags of spirits and cigarettes. I eventually make it to the luggage collection point and I tell him I am going to the loo and so he needs to watch our stuff. He wasn't listening.

Whilst washing my hands in the basin I let out a big sigh.

'You deserve better you know.'

I look to my left to see a woman about ten years my senior.

'Sorry?'

'I was sitting adjacent to your husband and that woman. Whilst you slept, well, he's disgusting and you deserve better. Get out before it's too late.'

She squeezed my upper arm and walked out. I let a tear run down my cheek.

When I left the bathroom, he was there struggling with the bags. We made eye contact and there it was. That look of pure anger. The look that said, 'Wait until I get you home.' *Great* I thought.

We made our way out of Heathrow and I insisted on buying us both a coffee. He didn't want one but I certainly did. His breath wreaked. *How many G&T's did he consume in two hours?*

We loaded the bags into the car and I drove us off. He was asleep within minutes. *Good.* It was tempting to take a long and very scenic route back.

We made it back home in good time. We live about an hour or so away on the south coast. He slept the whole way back and until I woke him up. Which I did about forty-five minutes after getting the bags out. He questioned why we had gotten back so late and I said I had stopped off for a snack on the drive back and left him snoozing in the car.

So far, no psycho outburst. It must be coming. I don't know what is taking him so long. Maybe he wants me to start making dinner so he can attack me with a frozen joint of lamb and then eat the evidence.

Ok perhaps that was a tad too far. Or maybe not. Most people who get murdered must not realise they are in the hands of a murderer otherwise they wouldn't go near them? Saying that, look at me. It started off great and now he tells me what I can and can't wear and when it's acceptable for me to look at my phone or go and see my friends. A psycho doesn't reveal themselves straight away. They lure you in, that's what makes them dangerous. Maybe he's a sociopath? I can't remember the difference. I will look it up on my phone at work tomorrow and then erase my search history before I get home.

Yes, I know what you are thinking and yes, he looks through my phone. Sometimes he does it in front of me and sometimes he does it when I'm in the shower. He will leave it open on something that wasn't the last thing I looked at just to let me know he has been in there. There is a password on it but he has that. Obviously when he first asked for it I did ask why and he just said that if I didn't have anything to hide then what was the problem. What was I supposed to answer to that? I didn't have anything to hide so I gave it to him. Now he looks at it all the time. I don't care, I've given up caring plus I don't have anything to hide. What annoys me more is when he takes it off me and says I am not allowed to look at it as we are having quality time together.

I don't answer my phone in front of him anymore. I am worried it that I will sound to happy when I'm talking to someone or that if the caller makes me laugh he will want to know every detail about the conversation. My friends don't get in touch anymore anyway. I never answer their calls and I take hours to respond to their texts so they don't bother with me. I catch up on their news on Facebook on my lunch break.

The evening was odd. Nothing was said about 'Penis – Gate' and if anything, he seemed to be trying to be nice. I pottered about sorting out all the washing as you do after a holiday and he put on the sports highlights and had a few beers. He ordered us an Indian take away, we watched a film and then we went to bed. He gave me a kiss goodnight and rolled over. He didn't try or ask for anything. Who knew. All I had to do was tell him I hate his penis and now he treats me with some kind of decency. Hopefully now we can live out the end of our days in a harmonious and sexless relationship.

Kalopsia

On a brighter note, I am back to work tomorrow and I can't wait. I am barely in the office. The UK Sales Director, Greg, is accompanying me on my client meetings and I think we are going somewhere for lunch. He only comes to our office for one week a month and I always look forward to his visits. He's a nice guy. Taken, as all the best ones seem to be. He's nice and he's funny so tomorrow will be a good day.

Chapter 4

I left earlier than I needed to this morning. Luckily, dickhead, sorry, Tom, doesn't have access to my work diary so I can lie about what time I leave and what time I will be finishing. If anything, I could've had a lie in this morning but I was awake at 5.30am. Once I was awake, there was no going back to sleep. Since our relationship began to plummet I have been waking up a lot earlier. The days seem so much longer, it's great! He doesn't notice because he doesn't get up until... actually, I don't know what time he gets up. He 'works when he wants to work' apparently so he gets up when he feels like it. He hasn't noticed that I have been getting up earlier so he must be sleeping until after a normal time that I would have left for the day.

My meeting is about a forty-minute drive away and Greg said he will meet me there. I was going to be far to early so I planned to stop off at the services for breakfast.

I pulled up in a parking space and turned off the ignition and the radio continued to play. I think it played for a minute before I decided that the song was shit and not helping my mood. I tried to yank my key out of the ignition but my fancy company BMW doesn't let you do that – you have to push the key in to pop it out. I began to push it in and out frantically which caused me to embark on a crusade of every swear word I know before it was finally released into my sweaty hand. I let out a deep sigh. For a moment, I thought I was going to start crying. I gave myself a pep talk and told myself to get some balls. There was no way I was going to be miserable at home and at work, I wouldn't let him take away the only thing that was mine. My job. I took out my emergency packet of cigarettes from the glove box and put them in my handbag and made my way into the service station to get my coffee.

I was going to sit in and have a healthy breakfast but that idea had gone. All I wanted was strong coffee and to chain smoke two cigarettes.

I chose to sit outside on a rancid, moss ridden, seagull shit covered, wooden bench. It looked filthy but I didn't care today. Bird shit or no bird shit, I was sitting down and I was having my coffee with a fag. No one could tell me what to do now, I was on my time.

Next to me was a table of what I can only assume where white van men. I don't mean to stereotype but you know what I mean. They all had navy blue cargo trousers on with heavy duty black boots and navy blue polo shirts. There was one who was clearly older. He was stocky, tattoos all up his arms and his hair shaved at the sides to remove the greys. You could tell that he wanted the lads to think he was cool but he also wanted to be taken seriously. As I came out of the building he smiled at me and then looked straight down at the ground. He pretended to blush. Have you ever seen that? When guys pretend to be coy? Cut the crap mate, I saw you swap your coffee cup to the hand with your wedding ring on that you tried to hide as you turned away from me. Then there was the scrawny one. The one who had less muscle than your average garden worm but more mouth than a rabid hyena.

'Alright darling?'

I said nothing as I sat down whilst they all stood there gawping.

'Oi darling, why the long face?'

'Oh, fuck off.'

'Oooh, she's a feisty one!'

I was not in the mood today but they all seemed to find something funny.

I perched on the bird shit riddled bench and turned so my back was to them and I was facing the wall of the building. I could see them in the reflection of the window. The third member of the male group who hadn't said anything seemed to be holding an imaginary figure, who I can only assume was meant to be me, and had me bent over whilst humping me like a sex deprived dog. I smirked as I saw it all in the window and they had no idea. Idiots. If that's his technique, then maybe I don't have it so bad at home.

I lit up my cancer stick and inhaled deeply. It felt good. It felt good because it was so wrong. My run after work tonight won't thank me for this but the Kate in the here and now thanks me for it. She thanks me for it because this Kate, is her own person and won't have her life ruled by Tom. Now that we are home and back from our mini – break in Barcelona, I have decided that we must definitely split. I just have to think of a way to do it with my life intact.

I was quietly puffing away on the very last bit of my cigarette planning my escape, mulling over various scenarios. I stood up having decided that one was more than enough and was stamping it out with my shiny, pointy stiletto which were possibly too high for work shoes when I saw Greg coming towards me. *Shit. Did he see me smoke? I bet he hates smokers. He doesn't know I smoke, hardly anyone does. I don't want him to know I smoke.* I riffled through my bag to look for perfume and quickly doused myself in it.

'Kate. Morning! Shall we?'

I had already begun walking with him back into the building without time to say that I had already had my coffee, he was leading the way. He opened the door for me and gestured for me to go in first.

I've got butterflies. Why do I have butterflies? Stop it Kate. He's the UK Sales Director with a team of three hundred staff beneath him and he has a wife. This is a rebound thing. Abort! Abort! He looks so good though. His smile is so nice and his shirt is so crisp. He's just… he's just lovely.

Before I knew it, we were in the McDonalds and he was ordering breakfast whilst asking me an array of questions about Barcelona but not actually allowing me to answer them. There was too much to do between deciding what to have for his breakfast, me waving the international signal for 'no thank you', the man taking the order and looking around for somewhere to sit.

Greg picks a table right at the back in the far corner and starts rambling again asking why am I there so early, how was my holiday, why I am not eating, tells me I have to eat and then begins to tell me that he has been to his father's care home this morning as he was called in about his Dad being 'inappropriate with an attractive, young carer.'

He finished his story at the same time he finished his breakfast and then said it was time to go. I hadn't really said a word but I didn't care. I enjoyed his company. He was so full of life, charismatic if you will and he was interesting.

I like him. Shit, I think I really like him.

We drove off in separate cars with him following me. I put on my sunglasses so that he couldn't see my eyes darting between the road and the rear-view mirror, looking at him. I liked him chasing me. That metaphor wasn't intended but it works. *Kate, stop it. You have trouble at home. You are looking for comfort. You do not like him. You don't fancy Greg. Sort your shit out.*

We arrive at our meeting which is with a manufacturing company to discuss their accounts. We work in the glamorous world of corporate finance. Everyone wants us on side, everyone wants to do a deal. I took the job as a stop gap. It has turned out to be the most lucrative job I have ever had. You wouldn't believe the amount of money there is in just keeping clients happy. I said I would do it for six months, I've been here for four years. The lovely Greg, sorry… Greg, has been with the company for ten years and usually visits our branch once a quarter but has been coming in monthly for the last few months. When he does, it brightens up my day. I noticed recently how disappointed I am when he leaves and I know I won't see him again for god knows how long. We are in contact regularly and I always sense a spark between us in our emails but perhaps he is like that with everyone. I have tried not to get too carried away with it.

I just like him. I don't fancy him or love him, I just think he is a great guy and I wish I could be with someone like him.

Greg himself is not the one for me but something similar would be good. Greg is somewhere in his forties, I don't know I have never asked. He has dark brown hair with flecks of grey throughout but it suits him. He has green eyes and very big eyes at that. I wish I had bigger eyes. Sorry, we were talking about Greg. He is a couple of inches taller than me, perfect heel height for kissing. *Kate, stop it!*

He looks like he has an athletic build under his suit if not slightly on the skinny side. The main thing is his humour. He's hilarious. He cracks me up every day to the point where people are now talking about it in the office. My team 'mates' all say I have a crush on him. I don't, I am just emotionally starved at home.

He led the meeting with me not really paying as much attention as I should have. I was too busy day dreaming about Greg's life and thinking how lucky his wife is. My wild and ludicrous train of thought was interrupted;

'What do you think, Kate?'

'I agree. It's a great deal. You should take it.'

We all smiled around the table and the Finance Director said;

'It is a good deal. We'll do it. Where do I sign?'

Greg looked at me, winked and under his breath, said;

'That's my girl.'

Alright, he didn't say that, he just smiled but I wish that's what he said.

We got the paperwork all signed off and Greg thanked them for their business.

'No, thank you, we are looking forward to winning some new business with these new improved loan rates'

'Oh, you won't be disappointed. We have the best rates going currently and my other accounts have been emailing me telling me how much business they are winning because of the cost saving they are able to show their customers.'

We all did a fake laugh as people do in these situations and my toes were curling with my 'cheesy work persona' but hey, if it works!

Outside the building Greg suggested we meet at a coffee shop around the corner to go over the meeting, of course I agreed. What happened next surprised me. Over a black coffee each, I ended up going into detail about how unhappy I was and told him how awful Tom is. He was shocked. I was shocked at how open I had been. He said that the relationship didn't sound healthy but he also said it would not be professional for him to advise me on how to handle it. I felt silly. Why had I told him? What made me open myself up to him like that? He didn't want to know. He was happy with his life. I am just a colleague to him. A colleague way down the pecking order for that matter.

I was confused. We went over the meeting. He told me what the buying signals were and how he overcame their objections. I took notes and pretended to give a shit. I didn't. I felt embarrassed for exposing my unhappy home life and wanted to leave.

We finished our coffees and as we were about to leave he grabbed my arm and I turned back.

'I have that dinner thing tonight. You know, the Finance Awards. Dave from head office emailed this morning and said he isn't coming. Do you want to come in his place? To represent the company?'

'I would love to... um... Tom will...I can't. Sorry.'

'I understand. It was short notice. See you tomorrow.'

I smiled, walked two steps and turned back again.

'Fuck Tom. I'll come. It's a work thing.'

'Only if you are sure?'

'Yes. Definitely.'

'Great. I'll get a taxi to pick you up at seven, text me your address. See you tonight.'

I walked off trying to not show the spring in my step.

The rest of my afternoon was spent trying to get inside of Greg's head which was impossible as I haven't mastered that desirable skill yet. I couldn't figure out if he had invited me because Dave from head Office had dropped out or was it something else? *Did Greg want to spend the evening with me?* I tried to go over the conversation and pick it apart for every 'sign' of his interest I could think of butI couldn't muster up a perfectly reasonable explanation. The first 'sign' was an obvious one. The invite. Why did he ask me today? Once he knew how unhappy I was with Tom, perhaps he realised that I may be available to him? On the other hand, Dave may have only just cancelled and he thought an evening out might cheer me up? Then again, I thought I made it clear that Tom doesn't let me out of his sight? Perhaps he wanted to 'rescue' me for the evening. Show me how a real man treats a woman. He can't show me because it is a work event not a date, Kate! God damn what does this mean!

Once I had finished my final meeting for the day I drove home to break the news to Tom that I would be out this evening. I also had the task of attempting to make myself look pretty, but not too pretty. Tom would not want me going out looking too pretty. The fact that I was going out anyway was going to be a problem enough on its own.

Surprise, surprise he's lying on the sofa half cut. It's amazing how this 'working when he wants to work' doesn't seem to extend the normal working hours that we all have to endure. He hasn't contributed any rent or money towards bills for the last eight months. Apparently 'the work isn't coming in right now.' I would imagine whatever brewery it was that he was in today will be doing ok.

'Tom, I have been asked to go to a work thing tonight.'

He stirs from his boozy slumber and looks at me with a pathetic naughty school boy type smile.

'Yeah that's fine babe. What time?'

'It starts around 7:30.'

'Ok I'll give you a lift and then wait for you in a pub. Where is it?'

'It's ok. Greg is picking me up in a taxi. It's likely to be an all evening kind of thing.'

'I said I will take you. Tell Greg you don't need a taxi. Where is it, for the second time.'

'It's at the new hotel in the city centre. The taxi is already booked I think.'

He stood up and squared up to me.

'Are you putting Greg before me. Cancel the fucking lift, I am taking you.'

He threw the TV remote across the room and went out onto the balcony to smoke, slamming the door for impact which made me jump.

I went through to the bedroom to get ready. I had to find an outfit that was like an evening gown but try not to look too dressed up otherwise Tom will undoubtedly ask me who am I trying to impress. I chose a navy, floor length, sleeveless, chiffon gown. There was no detail to it. It came in at the waist but other than that it was just a long, plain dress. I straightened my hair and just left it down. Nothing special about that. I kept my make-up natural and didn't wear any lip gloss. I couldn't really be any more understated. Hopefully that will be acceptable to his lordship.

'Who the fuck are you trying to impress?'

Tom is now in the bedroom and has another drink in his hand.

'I thought you said you were going to give me a lift? You're smashed.'

'Oh, fuck off Kate. I've only had a few. So, who is he? You haven't been asked out before and now you are dressing up as if you are going to get laid and don't want me to give you a lift. What the fuck am I meant to think. You know most blokes wouldn't put up with this shit? I'm not most blokes though. I won't have you telling your work I wouldn't let you out so you can go but next time, tell them you've got plans.'

He left the room and I sat down on the bed with a heavy heart. *I wish he wouldn't do this to me.* I wrote out a text to Greg telling him I will meet him down there. I would have much rather gone with him so that I wouldn't have to walk in on my own and navigate my way through the crowd of tuxedo's.

Reluctantly and with my life, I let Tom take me to the event. He was pissed. There is no way he should be driving.

Hopefully he will be pulled over and locked up for being way over the limit but that's unlikely. Maybe he could wrap us around a tree, killing himself instantly and I could walk free with barely a scratch.

Kate, he is still someone's son. All the way there, he drove like a lunatic, taking corners far too quickly causing me to be thrown around in my seat, held in only by my seat belt. He was in a foul mood and he was letting me know. We arrived at the hotel and he pulled up like a complete prick outside, skidding outside the doors for impact.

'There is a pub just down there on the corner. I will wait there for you. You've got one hour.'

'Tom, it's a sit down three course dinner with guest speakers. I am not going to be an hour. I will get a taxi home. Greg will sort it out.'

Tom took my jaw with his hand and gripped my face hard.

'Why do you have to be such a cunt, Kate. Why do you want me to be mad? Get the fuck out. I'm not waiting up for you.'

I got out of the car, shaking, but not looking back. I smoothed down my dress, put on my smile and elegantly walked towards the building. He was still parked there, watching me go in. To my delight, about twelve tuxedos watched me walk in, eyeballing me from head to toe and then I was greeted by Greg who sophisticatedly kissed me on both cheeks. It was then that I heard his car screech off at speed. *Good. Fuck off you prick.*

I was disappointed to find that I wasn't sitting on the same table as Greg. He was on the top table, he hadn't mentioned that to me earlier today. It became clear to me all of a sudden that I had only been invited because Dave from Head Office couldn't make it, so I suppose that answered all my questions that I had been pondering. How silly of me. I had been plonked in amongst nine other suits at a circular table who all worked in the finance sector. I could only assume that I was put there to network and make us some new contacts. I'm sure all the other dinner guests were perfectly nice men but I was beginning to feel that the grief I was going to get for this evening would hardly be worth it. We had taken it in turns to go around the table and introduce ourselves with the standard elevator pitch before we were interrupted or if I'm being honest, saved, by the first course coming out. Chicken liver parfait, bruschetta and a piece of orange peel for what was supposed to be a fancy plate decoration but in my mind if you can't eat it, what's the point. A bit like this evening really.

The top table had a guest speaker in the form of a retired cricketer who just happened to be the father in law of a partner at a top local law firm who were sponsoring the event. To be fair to him, he was quite an engaging speaker with just the right amount of wit and inspiration in his speech. It was probably written for him. I kept staring at Greg who was seated two seats along from him and was not playing ball with me. He didn't look at me once. *He must feel my eyes burning into him? Everyone knows when they are being stared at, surely?*

I really wanted him to catch me staring, just so that I could quickly look away and pretend to act all coy. It wasn't going to happen so I gave up and decided to get to know the rest of the table better. There was an insurance broker, a relationship director from a top bank, two solicitors and some others who weren't close enough for me to speak to. Of the 'gents' that I did get to speak to, I got the distinct feeling that none of them really gave a shit about what I did for work but probably had more connotations as to what I was like in bed. I did my best to be charming and not tell them how I really felt about their transparent conversation.

'So, Kate, it is Kate isn't it? What is it you do?'

'Yes, it is Kate. Kate Roberts and I am an account manager for TRC.'

'Oh really. Very good. Good for you.'

Oh, fuck off you condescending prick. I smile and take a sip of the disgusting wine that we all supposedly get two glasses of each but I don't think I can finish the one I have got, let alone force another one down. The company is hard enough to stomach let alone the cheap wine.

After the dinner of overcooked chicken leg, tasteless mash and frozen/re-heated veg and the pudding which was supposed to be sticky toffee pudding and custard, the food torture was over. The suits were well on their way to getting plastered and I was well on my way to a deeper depression. The other guests, of which there were about ten other tables of ten, were all mostly out of their seats and beginning to mingle. I was on my feet as soon as was politely possible and went to speak to an acquaintance I had spotted at the bar. Daniel from an international print firm who used us as their main company to finance their deals. He had the personality of a dialling tone but at least it would get me away from the 1970's, sorry I mean the table I was on and it would stop me pining for Greg.

Daniel was boring the hell out of me with his stories of collecting coins and telling me about the new and somewhat rare set that he has put out on his dining room French dresser much to his partner's despair, when I was startled by a hand at the bottom of my back and a shot of sambuca being lowered in front of my face.

I turned to see Greg looking at me with an intrepid smile.

'I thought you could do with a livener. How's it going? Hope you've made some friends!'

He clinked shot glasses with me and we necked them simultaneously.

'Thanks! I didn't have you down as a shot man.'

'There's a lot you don't know about me Kate. But that's for another time. Who's your friend?'

'Sorry, this is Daniel. He works for Cartwright and Lambert who are one of my biggest accounts thanks to Daniel's finance deals… We have spoken on the phone many times and met once or twice.'

'Ah yes, I thought I recognised you Daniel. I mainly meet with or speak to your peers but I have heard good things about you. Hope it's all going well there. Would you like a shot?'

'No thank you. I have an early start tomorrow in Brighton.'

'Blimey. Busy guy. No problem. Kate, shall we.'

With that, Greg had ushered me away from Daniel and over to a spot at the bar on our own. He ordered us another Sambuca each.

'Daniel collects coins apparently. He has them dating back to the sixties. He thinks that makes them old enough to be valuable. I think he may have a way to go yet. I just thought I should tell you before you thought he was more interesting than he is.'

'Oh, I could tell he's not interesting, that's why I took you away. You are interesting. I'm interested in Kate Roberts.'

What the hell does that mean?
'On three. One, two…'
We both downed the shots, winced at the strong taste of aniseed and then laughed whilst wiping our mouths.

'No more Greg! I have work in the morning. You shouldn't be encouraging me.'

'Oh, come on girl, I thought you could do with cheering up. From what you said earlier, you'll be in trouble at home anyway so might as well make it worthwhile. You'll be fine tomorrow. You're on target anyway so you can take it easy… but I didn't say that if anyone asks. I need to speak to Simon from KPS before he goes. I'll be back in five minutes. Get us a drink in. I'll have a pint.'

He left a twenty on the bar next to me whilst squeezing the top of my arm and winking at me. Pooft! Just like that, he was gone again. *He comes as quickly as he leaves and I just can't figure him out.*

The guests slowly began to leave, some of them with their dignity and others not so much. That's what always surprised me with these dinner do's, the fact that people would get so slaughtered when they are representing their brand and in front of potential new customers. Don't get me wrong, I was tipsy. I think being square can be just as damaging to your potential to make new clients as it can be to get hammered but there has to be restraint if you want to be taken seriously. That is my opinion anyway. Greg was heading back over. Heart begins to flutter, head feels light.

'Did you get me this?' he said picking up his pint.

'Yes, you told me to. In fact, you paid for it.'

'So where is yours?'

'I didn't. I have work to deal with tomorrow and Tom to deal with tonight.'

'What did you say to me earlier? 'Fuck Tom' wasn't it? I'm getting you a drink. Excuse me, can I have a glass of prosecco and two sambucas.'

'Ok, ok. I will have the prosecco but no more sambuca!'

Greg held both shots in his hands.

'Kate, I had you down as a lot more fun than this. Don't be a bore. If your boss gives you a sambuca, you take the sambuca. You are supposed to be showing me a wild time tonight! And don't worry about Tom, I will share a taxi back with you, see you in and all will be fine. I promise. Now drink!'

As we licked our lips from our third sambuca they closed the bar, much to my relief. Greg said he had a few more goodbyes to say and then we would get a taxi and so I stood loitering around waiting for his command. I watched him work the room with his flare. It seemed like everyone liked him. He knew most people here and everyone looked happy to talk to him. Everybody liked Greg, including me.

We jumped into a taxi and sat in the back together. I couldn't remember ever sitting this close to him but now that I was, I never wanted the taxi journey to end and I wanted to touch him. In my drunken haze, I began to tell him some more about how deeply unhappy I was with Tom. He told me I must get out. I said I wanted to have fun. I wanted to feel alive. *I wanted to touch him. I'm going for it. I am going to touch him.* I placed my hand on his knee and leaned into the corner of his shoulder. He didn't cuddle me but I definitely didn't feel him become awkward or pull away. He didn't know what I was doing and he was playing it safe.

The taxi pulled up outside of my house and I sat up realising that I had almost drifted off. I thanked him for seeing me home safely. *I don't want this to end. He needs to know how I feel.*

I took his head in my hand and pulled his face to mine and just pecked him on the cheek. I pulled away and made sure we were looking into each other's eyes.

'Thank you for inviting me out. It was fun. See you tomorrow.'

I opened the car door and got out.

'Goodnight Kate.'

He never took his eyes off me, even when I closed the house door he was looking right at me until we were out of sight.

Chapter 5

I woke up with a slightly fuzzy head but I was in a good mood. I was buzzing about seeing Greg. I knew I shouldn't be but a little bit of window shopping never harmed anyone. Tom was still in bed as usual but he was awake. I had made us both a coffee and he acknowledged it without speaking. He hadn't said anything about last night... yet. It would be coming, in one form or another.

I picked out a plain, modest blouse and then peered through the blinds to check the weather. It looked like it was going to be a nice day and so I picked out a plain black pencil skirt to wear with it. Then I pulled on my black opaque tights over my long, skinny legs and began to get dressed. The skirt was non-offensive. Not quite knee length but not a belt either. The blouse was conservative and my hair was pulled back into a neat pony tail.

'You really are a tart.'

Tom was now sitting upright in bed sipping his coffee.

Here we go.

'Tom, why do we have to do this every fucking morning. Every fucking morning you have a go at me. I am either not sexy enough for you or I am too sexy. It's a work outfit for fuck sake. I am not a tart nor do I dress like one. In fact, just fuck off!'

I slammed the bedroom door, grabbed my lunch and left for work, early. I was always early to work because I couldn't wait to get out of that house. Even though it was my house. Every single day he chips away at me and I refuse to pander to him. I have given up so much for him but it is never enough. He won't be happy until he has me locked away in a tower.

I arrived at the office as the cleaners were just leaving. I like this time of day. It was quiet, empty, peaceful and safe. I walked over to my desk and noticed that Greg was also in early, sitting in the spare office that floating staff use and now he was looking at me. Cue butterflies.

'Well aren't we both keen to drive the business forward? Morning boss! How's the head.'

'Morning Roberts. The head is not great, would've asked you to get us some breakfast if I knew you were going to be this early. Everything ok when you got in last night? You're alive at least...'

'Yeah it was fine. This morning however... Actually, don't worry. Coffee?'

'That would be great. Teachers pet. You know how I like it don't you?' He is smiling at me oddly and his eyes were glaring into mine.

'Of course. Strong and black... like your men.'

I laughed at my own joke and he shook his head.

'You are something else. I would tell you off but seeing as you are making my drink...'

I walked away feeling like he was staring at my arse.

Something was definitely brewing. I could feel it. We both knew that we would or never could act on it but the feeling was enough. I could tell he liked me. He liked my cheeky chatter and I liked his... I hadn't figured it out yet. He wasn't gorgeous but he wasn't bad looking either. He was ageing slightly, greying hair, about 5"11, regular build. He was funny but I didn't know much about his personality yet. *Perhaps it could be the authority factor but I'm not eighteen so I doubt that is it. It's probably just the attention. It can't be that because I get a lot of attention. Sorry, that sounds big headed but I do.* The attention is mainly from ageing overweight men but if I ever wanted an older, larger than life man there certainly seemed to be a few of them about.

Knowing that being around Greg made me giddy told me that Tom and I were definitely over. I wasn't scared of him so much recently. I couldn't care less if he met someone else. I knew I wouldn't miss him. The fact that I was beginning to enjoy Greg's company so much sealed the deal. I have always been a committed and loyal partner. As soon as my eye starts wandering I know it is over. I don't want Greg. He has just been placed in front of me as a sign. *I would like someone like Greg. I hope my next boyfriend is someone like Greg. I need someone who can make me laugh. I need a Greg but not this Greg.*

I took the coffee's over to our desks and was very disappointed to see that Carl from HR was now in his glass office with the door closed. I hated these glass offices. I am an easily distracted person and seeing people deep in conversation but not knowing what is being said makes me create my own scenarios and distracts me from doing my work. It's a bit like if you've ever stayed up late or got up really early and you watch one of your favourite programmes on TV and they have one of those people doing sign language along to it, I like to try and guess what bit they are at. Anyway, I don't care what Carl is talking to Greg about. I'm just pissed off he is in there. I was going to pretend to have an issue with a customer just so that I could sit in there and talk to him for a bit. Oh well, I suppose I will have to get on and do some of the work I am paid to do or I can make up a story for Carl and Greg. Greg saw me coming and stood up and opened his door.

'Sorry to interrupt. Coffee for Greg!'

'Where's mine then, Kate?' laughed Carl. I hate office jokes like that. There is always someone that says that when you make a drink or 'should you be eating that' when opening any sort of food packaging or 'big night?' if you are seen drinking water or taking a painkiller. I can't stand generic, boring, predictable office jokes.

'Yours is probably in the last place that your personality was seen. Good luck trying to find it.'

Carl's face looked heartbroken as I closed the glass door probably a tad too aggressively. *Maybe that was a bit harsh. Remember to pay him a compliment later.*

I sat down at my desk and was delighted to see that my computer that I had switched on almost fifteen minutes ago had almost fired up.

Not quite, but we were almost ready for action. It always amazes me with these large corporate companies. We sell money. As in, we lend money to companies who don't have it. Want a quick starting PC? Forget it. Turn up one minute late? You're fired. There is no love for the staff. What's this? An email from Greg.

'Are you sure you're ok? You know where I am if you need to talk.'

Ok, I take it back. Maybe there is love for the staff.

'I'm good, thanks for asking.'

I began to plod through my tedious stream of emails. Complaint after complaint after complaint. Urgent call needed. Billing c*ck up. No funds. Refund now. I hated this side of it. I had to go out and sell them their finance dreams knowing full well that our accounting system was a mess and they would never have the money when they needed it. It was such a headache. My favourite bit was being out on the road and going to visit clients. I hated the paperwork and politics. *One day I will get a job where someone can do all my admin for me.* The commission was great and the busier my diary, the less time I had to pick up the crap. The customer would get so cheesed off they would phone in with their complaint instead and so someone else would have to deal with it.

I began to prepare three packs for my days meetings and was talking out loud whilst doing so, 'Case reviews, newsletter, letter from director, samples, early commitment vouchers...'

'Are we ready Roberts? I'll drive.'

Greg walked past me carrying his blazer and briefcase. I was confused. He hadn't said he was coming and he doesn't normally accompany me on so many meetings. He accompanied me yesterday. *Odd.* As I walked out to his car I began to wonder why he was coming with me today. *Shit. Last night. I overstepped the mark. I kissed him on the cheek. I had touched his leg. I basically flirted with him the whole way home. He's going to fire me.*

'Jump in! Don't want to be late.'

'We won't be late. The meeting is in Brighton and we have got two and half hours to get there. Why are you coming? Is everything ok?'

'I thought we could spend some time together. I felt sorry for you last night, Roberts. I can tell things are tough at home so I thought we could grab some lunch in Brighton. If that's ok with you? Need to make sure my number one sales girl is happy at work at least.'

He smiled at me and I felt a flutter in my chest.

'Ok sounds great.'

I buckled up and we sped off in his very sporty BMW. Don't ask me what size, shape, model or spirit animal it is because I don't know. All I know is that it growled when he started it up and I was jerked back into my bucket style seat when he pulled away.

Over the next two hours we chatted away like we had known each other for years. Ok, we have known each other for almost two years but it was always in a working capacity. This time it was personal. He wanted to know how I met Tom, he wanted to know how long it was good for, he wanted to know when it went bad and why it went bad. He listened. That was a new experience for me. We spoke about me for a good hour and then we stopped off for a coffee and I saw his childish side.

He opened the door to the service station and just as I was about to walk through first he jumped in front and shut the door behind him and laughed hysterically behind the glass door. Then he opened it apologetically but with a schoolboy grin and insisted on buying me a mocha to make up for his childish sense of humour. I liked it. At least he had a sense of humour. We got to the till and were served by a very pretty Eastern European girl with a name badge telling us she was called Svetlana.

She was gorgeous and was certainly not destined to spend her life working in a service station coffee shop. Greg had stopped goofing around and became all serious in front of her, I suppose he was trying to appear sexy and mysterious. *Payback time.*

'I'm so glad that you are marrying my brother Steve. I am so psyched for the wedding!'

I delivered it in a sickly sweet enthusiastic voice, winked at him and walked off. His face went a beautiful shade of crimson red.

'Well played, Roberts. Well played. She was too young for me anyway.'

'Yeah right. Like you'd say no.'

'I'll have you know I'm a happily married man!'

Shame.

'Well ok let's not go too wild, I'm a married man.'

He's not happy…

I was left speechless by his last sentence and so I said nothing, obviously. What was there to say. I didn't want to tell him that I was sorry to hear that and that perhaps it was a blip. I didn't want to ask why he was unhappy. I didn't know what to say. Whatever was happening, we were getting to know each other. Things were different. We hadn't spoken about the client, the background to the meeting and why I was going there. There was no work talk. It had all been about Tom and I followed by some goofing around and now he announces he is not happy. *Maybe he feels he can talk to me because he knows I am not happy. That must be it.*

We arrived at the meeting, a tech design company in Brighton. They were looking for finance for some new infrastructure that they needed in order to expand. This would be an easy sale. Greg observed whilst I did my thing, asking lots of questions, finding a connection with the Finance Director. She had just got back from Northampton , her son lives there. For the purpose of this meeting my Grandad is now from Northampton . I used to love trips there as a child apparently… I haven't been for a while as I have been focusing on my career but I am going back up there with all the family next month for his 90th. He died six years ago. Don't judge me, I have bills to pay and she likes me so no harm done. It's not like I said I would pop in and see her son and drop off his mail to him.

'The fact is you are paying 6.3% APR and you are not meeting your repayments. Those prices are astronomical. I can settle off your existing agreement, reduce your costs and make you a saving of two thousand pounds per year. With a saving like that they should give you an extra day's holiday so you can have longer with your son next time. It's a great deal. You should take it.'

'Thank you, Kate. I didn't realise so much could be saved, I thought we were paying the going rate.'

'I'm sure you did and to be honest, if this was a multi-million pound business I might have charged more but you are a fairly new start up that is going places. You need the money to expand. It doesn't seem right making a profit when it comes to start ups, it just doesn't sit right with me. If you go ahead with my offer, I will have a nice romantic meal out with my husband with the small amount of commission and that will be enough for me.'

'Thank you so much Kate. Where do I sign?'

Back in the car Greg was smiling to himself and shaking his head in disbelief.

'You are brutal Kate! Northampton ? Husband? Wow!'

'We got a deal and she saves money. No harm done.'

I was playing it down but I was feeling pretty smug. I wanted him to see me in my element and I had done a good job. I oozed charm, even if I do say so myself.

'A meal out will do you? Kate, there was eight grand profit in that deal of which you will get sixteen hundred quid! That's a hell of a meal out. Priceless! Loving your work. Let's go for lunch to celebrate.'

We found ourselves at a funky jazz café come bar down on Brighton waterfront. It was buzzing even though it was a working day. Perhaps most of the people there had bunked off because it was such lovely weather. There was live jazz music and outdoor table service. What more could you want. A slender, bronzed and somewhat bohemian looking waitress arrived at our table. She was quite tall. So tall that her navel was my eye level. She had cut off denim shorts that hung low on her non-existent hips and was wearing a cropped t-shirt. I could see a tattoo of a mermaid wrapping itself around the front of her torso to the back. She looked cool. Our styles were very different but I can appreciate an attractive woman when I see one.

'Love the tattoo. It suits you.'

'Aw fanks babe. I like your curly hair.'

She didn't need to return my compliment with a compliment but I took it nonetheless. What is it with us brits not being able to deliver or receive compliments well? Someone said to me once, try to take a compliment by just saying 'thanks' and I find that very hard to do. When someone compliments me, I feel exposed in some sort of way. Almost naked to the eye. It's like they are studying me and I can't handle it with my highly self-critical personality.

'Two Americanos please.'

'Oh, not for me, I've had my coffee quota for the day. Please can I have a green tea?'

'Oh yeah great. Make that two. I love green tea. My wife hates it but then she hates most of the things I like. It's a healthy marriage!'

I couldn't tell if he was joking or not. A lot of people joke about their marriages. More marriages are unhappy than not. I can name one couple who are good friends of mine who adore each other and it is truly beautiful to see. The others, mostly they all love each other but are they all happy? I don't think so. Most would change some parts if not most parts to their partner's genetic make-up, some I think are stuck in a rut and are just plodding along. Sadly, I think some have 'settled' as it were but what I do know is that they all joke about 'the ball and chain' or 'her/him indoors'. So, when presented with a boss that I am finding more attractive by the minute who seems to be taking more of an interest in me and is now eluding to being in an unhappy marriage, what does he want me to think.

'Sounds pretty healthy to me, Greg. Who am I to judge. If your only problem is that you both like different hot drink's then I think you've got it made. Anyway, where are the menus?'

'I'll grab some, I want to wash my hands anyway.'

He got up and left the table and I watched him walked in to the bar and get smaller and further away from me. *He has a great arse. Stop it!*

His phone started ringing and the name Kirsty flashed up on it. *I wonder if Kirsty is the wife? I bet she is calling to see what he wants for dinner or maybe just to tell him she loves him.* My mind pondered who

Kirsty was and what she might look like and why she was calling. Then a text flashed up but I could only make out the first line, 'Don't bother coming home tonight you wa...' *That's annoying. I want to know what the rest says. What begins with wa? Wanker? Ooh a falling out. In-ter-es-ting.*

'Hey, here we go. Two menus. I'm feeling quite peckish now actually.'

'Thanks. Me too. I think your phone was ringing by the way.'

Greg picked up his phone, briefly looked at the screen and dismissed it without so much as even a flicker in his eye. *The plot thickens.*

'No one important. Now what shall we have, do you fancy sharing something?'

No one important and do I want to share? He is definitely trying to make this an intimate meeting. It's not normal to share lunch with your boss, is it?

'Sounds great.'

We spent way more than our allocated one hour lunch break in the beach bar. The afternoon passed with the refreshing sea breeze and glorious sizzling sun. The faint melody of a lone jazz musician drifting off towards the horizon. Greg was funny. We spent a couple of hours laughing as he told me amusing stories ranging from his student days, to recent boozy escapades with his friends, his joys of being a father. He was incredibly open. Greg had been more open with me in two hours than Tom had been in two years. He let me in and that's what it felt like, like I was going in. I was slowly being drawn into Greg's world and I wanted more. I couldn't remember if I had ever spoken to a man who had shared his thoughts and feelings with me like that before. Not a word was spoken about work, we were like two friends just having a good time together. Eventually the bubble had to be burst.

'Right come on you, I'll get the bill and we had better head back.'

My heart sank. I didn't want to go. I didn't want to go back to work and I didn't want to go back to Tom. I suddenly felt sad and depressed. As if the high was wearing off with a dramatic drop.

The drive back went quicker than I had hoped and most of it was spent with Greg speaking to clients on hands free so we didn't really get to talk. He dropped me off at my car which was parked around the corner from the office and congratulated me on a great deal earlier that day. He was still on a call as he waved goodbye and sped off. It was odd. When we were having lunch, he made me feel like I was the only girl in the world and now he had dropped me off without ending his call and drove away without so much as a second glance. The joy ride was over.

Chapter 6

The weekend was upon us and it was our turn to have Tom's daughter. I preferred it these days when she was over. Admittedly, in the early days it was difficult at times when Cara visited as having not had any of my own children I wanted to be able to do what I wanted, when I wanted. I didn't expect that I would have to give up my freedoms for someone else's kid. I was happy to get involved and spend time together but I didn't realise I was going to become a step mum so quickly. I wondered occasionally if Tom had deliberately sought out that position to be filled. As time went on I didn't believe his demands were for nurturing reasons either. I believed it was because he resented having his freedoms taken away from him and wanted to make someone as trapped as he felt.

Tom and I would argue because he would say that it wasn't fair if I made plans with my friends on the weekends he had his daughter because he couldn't make plans. I tried to explain to him that he was Cara's dad and that as I wasn't her parent, I didn't have to commit my free time to her. These conversations started when we were only about eight months in to our relationship together. I should've seen the signs.

My friends all told me how out of order he was. 'Kate come out for drinks tonight!' They would demand most weekends.

'I can't. We have Cara this weekend' I would text back with a heavy heart.

'So! She's not your kid. Tell Tom to fuck off.'

If only I could. Tom told me how unreasonable I was and how selfish I was and said I wouldn't last five minutes if I had my own kid. He said if I wanted a kid with him then I had to prove myself to him with the one he had. His five year-old daughter. How could I demonstrate how I could care for an infant when his child was, well, was his child and we saw her once every two weeks? The rows became worse and more ferocious. I didn't feel that I was in the wrong and all my friends told me he was in the wrong but eventually I succumbed. I thought if I tried harder to keep him happy then he might become happier and start being nicer. He was like the nursery rhyme; When he was good he was very, very good but when he was a shit he was a mighty shit.

I gave in or should I say gave up a little more of me for him. I agreed that when we had Cara I wouldn't make any plans for the whole weekend. That was Thursday after school through to Monday morning. Cara was eight. All she wanted to do was play with us and have her Dad's constant attention so to save any more hostility, I agreed to sit in with Tom whenever we had Cara over to stay at my house.

Admittedly, since I began making more of an effort, Cara and mine's relationship blossomed. She knew her Dad was an arse and she knew her Dad was an arse to me, despite how young she was. She loved her Dad very much and looked up to him but she wasn't stupid. I insisted that she should not be left to watch TV all the time and should be more engaged in activities with us. It was a risky move but it paid off. It turned out that Cara liked to cook. She would help me prepare the veg whilst I prepared the meat and usually she would hang around in the kitchen and talk to me about her life. She hated her mother's new boyfriend. I encouraged her to get to know him and to try and not give her Mum a hard time. Tom encouraged her to give her Mum a hard time. They would both criticise Brian, the boyfriend, who by all accounts didn't have much of a personality and Tom and Cara had both decided he was a loser. God knows what was said about me when I was first on the scene. Hopefully Laura, the ex, was fair when asked.

Kalopsia

I did not approve of them slagging neither Laura or Brian and I told him so. Tom knew I was right and that was why he wanted me to be around Cara, so that I could take over the parenting role and do a better job of it than him. I could tell that Cara only joined in on the slagging matches because she wanted to make her Dad happy and was constantly looking for her Dad to invest some time in her and the only time she got with Tom was mainly when he was slagging off his ex-wife Laura and her new partner Brian.

Brian was not Cara's kind of guy and I appreciate that it was easier for us to be friends what with me being much younger than Tom but still, respect begins from infancy and if Cara looked up to her Dad then she was going to need all the help she could get.

It was Saturday morning and it looked like it was going to be a beautiful day. Cara was already up and eating cereal on the sofa much to my annoyance. I got up and made some filter coffee and took a mug through to Tom in bed. I remember sleeping in at the weekends but these days I seemed to be up at the crack of dawn.

'Why don't we take Cara to the beach today? I can make us up a picnic?'

'Oh god babe, I can't be arsed. I've had a busy week.' *Has he? This is news to me.*

'Oh, Tom come on! It's lovely outside, look!' I drew open the curtains and the bright early summer sun flooded the room with light.

'Come 'ere you. Get back into bed.'

I gingerly crept back into bed knowing where this could be leading knowing full well that I was not in the slightest bit interested. I kept hold of my mug the whole time as a preventative from any quick movements. He slapped my thigh and began stroking it with each stroke going further and further up my leg. My body clenched as if someone had placed a python on me and the only way to get out alive was to remain deadly still.

'Tom, Cara is next door. She could come in at any minute.' I took his hand and entwined our fingers. Tom rolled over and took my coffee cup away from me. *Oh god, please no. Please, get off.* He pulled my silk dressing gown apart to expose my breasts and began kissing my neck and chest.

'Tom!' I pretended to giggle but what I was attempting to do was make enough noise to make Cara aware that we were up and then she would be in our room within minutes asking what we were doing that day.

'Shh' he said, planting kisses on my body and working his way down lower and lower. I let out a shriek of impersonated pleasure. Then I heard the thud. *Hallelujah! I could punch the air right now.* The thud was Cara leaping off the sofa because my laugh had startled her. Right now, she was putting her cereal bowl in the kitchen and in about one minute she would knock the door and open it without being told to come in. I knew it. Tom knew it. I heard the clank of dishes in the kitchen and Tom sat up in bed pulling the covers over us both and picking up his coffee. *Sweet, sweet victory.*

'Morning Daddy. Morning Kate. What are we doing today?'

'Well I was just saying to your Dad that we should go to the beach. I could make up a picnic.'

'Yeah can we! Can I take my bucket and spade? Shall I go and get everything out of the shed and put it in the boot?'

'Just go and watch TV and then we can get sorted.' Cara looked genuinely satisfied as she left the room in a sleepy haze.

'Fuck sake Kate. I said I didn't want to.'

'Oh, come on grumpy bones. Look how happy she was at the idea. It won't kill you and you should do stuff with her, get her away from that TV. Plus, if you don't, you know who will don't you? Brian.'

'Brian is not taking my daughter to the beach.' He rolled over, took my mug away from me again and made his intentions known.

'Cara is having breakfast, we've got a few minutes.' *As long as that? Great.*

Whilst showering, trying to remove Tom's residue from the two minutes of torture I had just played along with and keeping down the strong desire to be violently sick, I could hear the lively movements of a very excited eight year old getting ready for a day out with her Dad.

All she wanted was to be her Daddy's little girl yet Tom the selfish prick didn't even seem to want to make his daughter happy. *Why is he so moody?* The only time he made a genuine effort with Cara was to compete with Laura. If she bought her something, Tom would go out and buy the same thing at three times the cost. If she took her to Thorpe Park he would take her to Alton Towers and stay in the hotel there for two nights. He was a man child, through and through. If anyone had to prove themselves to be parent material it was him.

After my shower, I said I would nip to the supermarket to get picnic essentials. Cara asked if I could drop her off at her Mum's to get some bits which was fine by me and then Tom piped up that I could drop him to the pub. It was 10:30am.

'Tom, I am going to be fifteen minutes. There isn't time for the pub.'

'I'll just have a swift one. That's a perfect amount of time.'

'You aren't going to let Cara down are you? Just the one, yes?'

'Yes Kate, just the one. Take me to the pub, her to her Mum's, she can walk to the pub once she's got her stuff and you can pick us both up.' There was no point arguing. He has a drink problem but won't admit it. At least this way I can get rid of him for a bit.

We all got in the car and I dropped Tom to the pub at 10.57am. The landlady was just opening the doors. *How embarrassing.* She waved at us and I gave her an awkward smile. Tom was placing his order with her before he had even got both feet out of the car. I told him I wouldn't be long and dropped the alcoholic off to his real love.

'Kate, can I come to the shop with you?'

'Yeah of course, if you want to. I thought you hated supermarkets though?'

'I do but I don't mind going with you. Dad never wants me anywhere. You're nice so I don't mind walking around with you. Plus, there is a magazine I want if you don't mind.'

My heart melted. She was a sweet girl and Tom didn't deserve her.

'Of course you can come with me and take no notice of your Dad. You know how much he likes a beer. As a treat for keeping me company, I will let you pick out any three items that you want for the picnic. Anything. I won't complain about how bad they are for you.'

We both smiled at each other and pulled up into the car park. We quickly whizzed around the supermarket and grabbed lots of goodies and convenience food. Cara wasn't the only one who hated food shopping. I don't like shopping in general really. I only go when there is something I want or need. It seems to me that some people actually go food shopping as an activity. They doddle, usually in front of me and spend ages at shelves umming and arring over what version they want of the item they are trying to choose. Sometimes I would like to snatch it out of their hand, chuck it in to their trolley and say 'just bloody get it. There is a whole world outside you know.'

Anyway, with a basket laden with snacks that would definitely put a layer of fat in the lining of our arteries we were almost good to go. All that would require making would be sandwiches or rolls. We were lucky enough to grab a till where someone was just paying up. Small things like that make my day. No queuing around with people wearing onesies and slippers. Supermarkets = god awful places. Cara packed the bags, not the way I would have done it but the items were going straight in the boot of the car so I didn't care and yes, before you have a go at me, I appreciated her help. I'm just particular about how I like my bags packed ok? Freezer bag, fridge bag, cupboard bag, bathroom bag. You get the idea. It makes it easier for unpacking.

I pulled up outside the pub and Tom was now sat with a few of the locals who religiously attended the joint as well.

'Go and grab your Dad and tell him we are ready.' Cara hopped out and I saw her talking to Tom and then walking back to the car on her own. *What the fuck now?*

'Dad has just got one in. He said come and join him. Do we have to? It's boring.'

'No, we don't have to. I knew he would do this. I'll go and speak to him.' I got out of the car and walked over to the men wearing my best false smile.

'Hi everyone. Tom, you said to come and get you. We are ready.'

'Well I'm not. Look.' He pointed to his beer and smiled at me like a muppet. 'Have one babe, I'll get you one in. What do you want?'

'I can't. All the food is in the boot.'

'Yeah well we will go to the beach straight after this. Just have one.'

'We can't go straight to the beach. I haven't made the rolls and we need to pick up the stuff Cara wants from her Mum's.'

'Well why did you come to get me if you're not ready? That was stupid. Go and get ready and then come and get me.'

I smiled through gritted teeth and left the silent table. I wondered if they all knew he was a prick to me or did they think I was a nagging girlfriend and I should leave him to his beer.

I got back in the car and Cara looked genuinely disappointed. She had big blue eyes. Although she was eight, she was wise beyond her years but still looked cute. Not that I would tell her that, she's far too cool to be cute.

'We are going to the beach, aren't we Kate?'

'Of course we are. Your Dad promised. We are going to go back. I will make some rolls whilst you get your stuff from your Mum's and then I will pick you up and we will go.'

As his Lordship had requested, we went back home and got everything ready and by the time we got to the pub he had… you guessed it… just got another one in. This was his third pint and it was just before noon. Cara and I had no option but to have one with him so I had half a cider and Cara begrudgingly had a Pepsi.

About thirty minutes later we were finally ready to go. The change in Cara was clearly visible when the three of us were in the car and off to the beach. I don't expect Tom to run rings around the girl but we don't have to do it every weekend and her only other interest is dolls. If we can get her outside and willing to do something then that needs to be encouraged. Tom just doesn't like doing anything for anyone else.

The two of them picked up the blankets and went to go and find a spot whilst I loaded myself up with picnic essentials and said I would find them. I was only about five minutes behind them. I spotted where they were pitching up and could see them together. Cara loved her Dad so much. It was so nice to see them together doing father and daughter things. I arrived and laid out the blanket. I got out the plastic cups and poured everyone a drink. Tom lay down on the blanket as soon as I put it there. I gathered a selection of treats for Cara and offered them to her. I tried to take an interest in what she was doing but I was afraid that I was clueless when it came to this sort of thing.

'So, how was school this week?'

'Yeah it was ok.'

'What did you learn about?'

'Stuff. Safety online.'

'Oh right. Do you think you know how to be safe online?'

'Yeah it's alright. Dad are you going to build a sand castle with me then? Dad?' Cara looked over her shoulder at where her doting father had plonked himself.

The bastard was asleep.

Chapter 7

Ok, so over the weekend things took a funny turn. Not with dickhead, sorry, Tom. With Greg. He sent me a text at 10.37pm on Saturday night. Surely, it's not normal for a boss to text an employee on the evening of a weekend? Let me tell you the details. The text read, 'Hey Roberts, how's your Saturday evening going? I've had a boozy one and the night is still going strong. Anyway, I've been told that two people from our office need to go to a corporate summer ball and so I choose you! I'll tell you the details on Monday. G x'

Tell me that there isn't something odd about that text? Ok never mind odd, that was far more relaxed than the sort of text I would expect from my boss. But I liked it. Luckily, Tom didn't see. He did ask who was texting me at that time of night and naturally, I lied. I wouldn't have done if I didn't think it would open up a whole new world of pain for me. I probably didn't need to lie to the extent I did to be fair. I had told him it was one of the girls and that they were asking me to come into town for drinks but that I had declined as I was much happier at home with him and Cara. He bought it and I bought my peace for an evening.

I did text Greg back. I didn't even think twice and part of me wished I had taken my time and thought of something more interesting to write. Instead, in my mad teenage-like love struck frenzy I quickly replied with; 'Sounds good. Looking forward to hearing more on Monday. K :)'

I didn't put a kiss so I'm not guilty of anything. He put a kiss for me but I had decided it was because he was pissed. He probably always puts a kiss at the end of a text for his wife and so he must've accidentally put one on for me, forgetting for a moment who he was texting. Anyway, he won't be texting me again with the mundane reply that I offered him.

As for Tom and I, the weekend passed without any real drama. The football was on all weekend so that worked for us all. He sat around drinking all day and watching the football whilst I kept him topped up with booze, snacks and meals. I even earned some brownie points by playing with Cara on her Xbox for a while. I am crap at computer games but I would rather that than watch football. Cara surprises me. When I was her age, I wouldn't be asking for any parent, bio or step, to play computer games with me. I wanted them to leave me alone but she had asked me several times and I felt that I owed it to her. I couldn't say no again. She tried to teach me how to ride a pony but not only is it not easy in the real world, it's much harder in the virtual world. Mounting a horse on these games seemed like trying to climb a waterfall or something. The slightest push of a button for a lift of the foot to get into the stirrups had me falling off into the dirt which Cara thought was hilarious. Cara told me with conviction that she knew he would be an excellent horse rider because she was so good on this game. *Good luck with that little lady.*

All in all, it was a quiet weekend. I got all our washing and ironing done and most importantly, Cara's school stuff prepped and ready. I did my nails and other girly things like wore a face mask, washed and straightened my hair which believe me is a lengthy and tedious task. You have to be prepared for heavy aching arms and a lot of patience. All that just to have it frizz up as soon as you step outside but variety is the spice of life as they say. Sometimes it was nice to get on and do these things without being rushed. The added bonus being that Tom was glued to the TV all weekend so I was left in peace to get on with it.

Monday arrived and Cara and I left for school and work whilst Tom was still asleep. Bliss. A non-eventful weekend followed by a pain-free

Monday morning. No comments about my clothes. No waking up in a bad mood and giving me shit. Pure bliss.

I pulled up outside Cara's school and wished her a good day. We had chatted pleasantries on the way in. Another thing that impressed me about this girl was that she wouldn't moan or grumble about going to school. She was a cup half full kind of kid. We kissed each other on the cheek and just as she got out of the car, she leaned in and said,

'I'm so glad Dad has you Kate. He'd be even more miserable without you.' She shut the door and walked off without giving me time to respond. I felt the guilt flood my body. She was such a good kid and I had been aware for the last few months that one of the reasons I hadn't ended it with Tom yet was because of Cara. I had grown to care for her much more than I ever expected to and I was beginning to enjoy being her step-mum. I knew she would be gutted it we separated but I also knew that was not a reason to stay.

As I arrived at work that morning my good mood was instantly flattened by realising that Greg was not in. If he wasn't in early it was likely he might not be in at all. *His text said we would talk about that event today. Where is he?* I knew it was none of my business where he was and that he didn't owe me anything but my despair with Tom made me feel extremely needy for anything good. Greg made me feel good. I always looked forward to seeing him knowing that he would make me laugh.

The Monday mood seeped in and I was thoroughly pissed off. Greg's visits to our office made this job. Without his charisma, this was a dull place to work. Then my phone beeped to tell me I had a text.

'Fancy meeting me for lunch? I'm not in your office today but am meeting a client. G x'

A burst of happiness exploded within me. Something akin to a unicorn throwing up glitter all over me. The unicorn effect was so instant and so effective. Happy Kate again. *Don't text back right away. Don't be an idiot, text him back! Maybe it's a test, I am supposed to be working. It's not a test. He wants me. Oh, for god sake. Just send a ruddy text.*

'Hey piss head, wondered where you were. I was expecting the summer ball itinerary. Lunch sounds good. Where?' Sent. *Shit, shouldn't have called him a piss head. What if he is offended? Mind you, he was the one that told me he was boozing it up on Saturday night.* Ping! Another text came in.

'Who are you calling piss head? I'm still your boss young lady. Don't make me give you a dressing down ;) The Chapel Arms in Sandbridge. 1pm. See you then. Be good. G x'

I don't care what anyone says. Things are now definitely taking a turn in the unprofessional direction but I don't seem to mind. I know the dangers. I know what's right and wrong but I want to know more about him. He has caught my interest and now I can't stop thinking about him. Ping! *He is keen! Oh, it's Tom. Ignore.*

The morning went by and nothing could dampen my mood. Tom tried to call twice and sent another text. I didn't look at them let alone respond. This was the one place where I could get away with ignoring him. For all he knows I am busy. I'm not busy. It's Monday morning. Everyone has been talking about their weekend and sharing their boozy stories. Most of my colleagues are young men who live to party at the weekends. Andy did the Starbucks run on the way in and bought everyone a coffee. Alan was setting up his indoor golf set and the Monday morning tomfoolery was under way. Whilst the boss is away…

Talking of the boss, ping!

'Hope you're working hard? What's Andy up to? Is he hungover? G x'

'I would be working hard but my phone keeps going off ;) Everyone is working… that's the right answer, yeah? K x'

'I don't mind you looking at your phone to text me, as long as it's not your loser boyfriend ;) G x'

What the hell just happened? He is texting me with kisses, inviting me out to lunch and now he's calling Tom a loser. *Hmmm.* In between joining in with all the office high-jinx I had been constantly clock watching. As soon as it reached 12:15pm I was out of here and off to explore what was happening with me and my boss.

I had put a fake appointment in my online diary to cover my absence and packed up my laptop and notepad. I didn't know how long this 'lunch' was going to go on for. As I said goodbye to my colleagues, Tom appeared. *Shit.*

He walked in to the office with a very clear, but not visible, chip on his shoulder. All the boys stopped what they were doing and acknowledged him with a chorus of 'alright mate' which was delivered with different levels of enthusiasm but with an all-round undertone of 'we couldn't give a shit if you respond or not'. Tom gave them an upward nod of the head rather than an actual verbal greeting. He really thought he was the dog's bollocks sometimes. It was embarrassing.

'Hey, what are you doing here?'

'That's no way to speak to your fiancé is it now? Where's my kiss?'

Stop embarrassing me. 'I'm just heading out, I've got a meeting to go to.'

'At lunch time? What about lunch?' He started looking moody as if he knew I was meeting someone for lunch.

'I've got to go to Brighton, I need to be there for 2.30pm and I'm going to be late if I don't go now. Sorry, I didn't know you were coming in.'

'Well if you had looked at your phone you would know. Forget it, I was only trying to be nice. Don't know why I bother.' He was almost out of sight by the time he had finished his sentence. He got in to his car and sped off whilst the rest of the office just looked at me. Someone said, 'what a jumped-up prick' but I'm not actually sure who said it. Embarrassed, I picked up my things and left. As I got in to my car I was paranoid that he would be following me and discover that I am having lunch with Greg and then I would be dead meat. *I haven't done anything though and I am entitled to lunch. I never know where he is or what he's doing and heaven forbid I ask.*

I decided to take the gamble. I wanted to have lunch with Greg and although I wasn't exactly sure as to why we were really having lunch it was none of Tom's business. The amount of times I have caught him deleting texts or ignoring calls. I have never caught him with his pants down but I've been close enough. I was going to have lunch with Greg and if he followed me and caused a scene, I could use that as my opportunity to end things with him. I had been looking for opportunities to end things for months but then we could have a nice day or weekend together and I would wonder if it was all my fault. I also reminded myself that the grass was never greener. I arrived at the Chapel Arms and Greg was already there and sitting at a table outside in clear view for me to see as I pulled up in the car park. What happened next was odd.

We spent the afternoon talking only about work and going over my pipeline and prospects. I was glad I had brought my work things with me otherwise it could've been pretty embarrassing. He wanted to know my sales forecast, he wanted to know what appointments I had been on and what probability I had of converting them. The time we spent together was purely professional and above board. Apart from me looking at the tuft of hair emanating from the undone button of his shirt and wondering what the rest of his torso looked like and being slightly aroused by that thought. I daren't bring up the texts or go off the course of conversation we were having. *Maybe that is just his way. Maybe I have read this all wrong.*

'Well you had better skedaddle. I think we have talked enough work for one day. It's Monday, no one likes Monday's but the sun is shining. Take yourself home for an early finish.'

'Thanks Greg, are you sure?'

'I'm sure you shouldn't be questioning it. Go on, clear off before my wife arrives. I don't want her thinking we are having an affair.'

'Roger that. You don't need to tell me twice. Have a great rest of the afternoon.' As I picked up all my things consumed by disappointment that he was having a date night I said goodbye and he winked at me. My whole stomach flipped. I didn't know a one eye wink could do that to someone. It's been ages since anyone winked at me so I couldn't remember if that always happened or was it because it was him that did it? Deep down I knew it was because he did it. Who was I kidding. I needed to get a grip and move on from this silly school girl crush. He wasn't even that hot.

I made my way back through the blistering heat and the tediously slow, backed up traffic going over as much as the conversation as I could remember. I had plenty of time to think as it would seem that everyone had left work early and I was crawling along the dual carriageway. It was on days like today that I was super glad I had invested in a soft top sports car last summer. There were times when I hugely regretted it, like when the huge direct debit came out of my account every month but at the time I thought these could be my last few years without kids so I should seize the impracticality and make the most of it. The roof was down, the sun was on my skin and many overweight, shirt drenched, old enough to be my Dad business like men couldn't resist taking a peek as they crawled past. Ok, that was another time when I regretted having it. With the roof down I felt so exposed which was ok if it was the right spectator but when it was Gordon Brown lookalikes I would find myself sinking into my seat and pulling my skirt down as far as the fabric could make it towards my knees.

What had got me was why would his wife think he was having an affair if she saw him with me? We are colleagues. I wondered if he told me about him meeting his wife there as he knew my mind had been running away with me and he wanted to make it clear it was just a bit of fun? *But those texts. They weren't your average boss texts.*

My mind was a complete muddle as I drove back. What I had realised was that whatever was happening, this could be a dangerous tryst. Not only because we are both in relationships but he can go from making me feel elated to devastated within seconds. Only one other has done that to me before and that was my first love Nick. It took me a long time to get over him and I told myself that I would never love another as deeply as that again. Nick knew I was putty in his hands. I was seventeen and young and naïve and he exploited every aspect of me. Greg had the same power over me. I could feel it. I knew how bad it was for me and yet I wanted to find out more. D day was looming for Tom and I. D for dumped. I might be many things but I am not a cheat and theoretically, in my head, I am already cheating on him.

Chapter 8

Things had been strange at home that week. Tom had been incredibly nice and helpful. Completely out of character for him and somewhat reminiscent of our earlier days together. I didn't care. That ship had sailed. Nothing he could do could bring us back to shore now. I was just trying to find my moment. He had cooked my favourite meals, dinner had been waiting every night I had come home. He had poured me a wine every evening, asked me what I wanted to do with our time together, asked if I wanted to pick a film to watch. He had even spent less time in the pub. Although apparently, he had had a clash with Marcus in there and was giving him a wide birth. When I quizzed him as to what that was about he said that Marcus was 'just being his usual twatty self.' I expected that there was more to that story but couldn't be bothered to ask and didn't really care.

The week rolled into the weekend and I made plans to catch up with friends. I did this to rouse Tom and create an argument. We didn't have Cara this weekend so it was an ideal dumping window. I just wanted him to have a go at me and then I could dump him and make it out to be all his fault which is was. He didn't bite though. He must've sensed that something was brewing and he was clinging on. I tried every trick in the book to piss him off without being a complete bitch. I didn't finish a single meal he had made. When he asked how it was I would play with the leftovers and tell him it was 'alright, not your best' and when he tried to cuddle up on the sofa I would tell him I was too hot. I had a headache all weekend at bedtime. He didn't say a word. Not once. He just became nicer and nicer.

On Sunday evening, I made my excuses for an early night and told him to stay up and watch his programme as I 'still wasn't feeling great'. He allowed me my request but this time his eyes looked like a scolded puppy. He knew something was up. He knew I was gone. He knew it was just a matter of time. I felt like shit. I hated hurting people. Despite all the pain he had caused me, I still didn't want to hurt him. Despite the times he would go missing on a night out with the boys and 'stay at Dave's mates house', despite my friends finding him on dating websites, despite him blowing loads of money in strip clubs, despite him having a load of female friends that I never got to meet, despite him trying to control me and shape me into a frumpy house wife, despite him throwing out my clothes that he didn't like, despite him looking at my phone constantly. That's not everything but despite all of that, seeing that look in his eyes made me feel like utter shit. *Just rip the plaster off, Kate.* Ping! A text had come in.

'Dress nice tomorrow, we are going to a drinks reception tomorrow night. G x'

'How nice is dress nice? Where are we going? K x'

'A client's summer drinks reception, wear a cocktail dress. I'll tell you more tomorrow. G x'

'Ok. Sounds good. K x'

I set my alarm for 6.30am. My heart was racing. We were back on and my feelings for guilt over Tom were off. I can't believe what this man was capable of doing to me. *Be careful Kate. Be very careful.* Ping!

'Sweet dreams. G x' *Ok we are on. We are very much on.*

I instantly felt excited by what was brewing. He wanted me and I wanted him. We both knew it. I know it's wrong but I went through to the living room and straddled Tom in my silk dressing gown. I needed sex now and I wanted it to be with Greg but for now I would make do with Tom. Tom didn't know what had hit him. My performance that evening was similar to that of a porn star. It was so good that Tom only lasted three thrusts and it was all over. My made-up fantasy of me and Greg was over. I tried so hard to picture Greg in my head but it wasn't that good. I kissed Tom and he smiled and picked up the TV remote. He was happy as a pig in... well you know. I, however, was not. I went to the bathroom and finished off what Tom couldn't. I wonder what Greg is like, down there? My time in the bathroom didn't take long either. I craved Greg like I had never craved a man before. Was it because he was my boss? Did I really fancy him? What about his wife? *I can't get with a married man, then again, it's his marriage not mine. No Kate, no! You are not that girl!*

My alarm went off at 6.30am and I bounded out of bed. I literally couldn't wait to see Greg and get away from Tom. Tom rolled over this time all bleary eyed and looking happy with himself.

'You were a little minx last night. I almost thought I'd lost you. Turns out I've still got it.'

I walked out the room. I don't know why. I had never done that before. I left him there hanging without saying a word and just closed the door. That was mean but I couldn't look at him. I couldn't face him. If that wasn't a signal to him then who knows what was. I didn't care. I would deal with him later. Right now, I just wanted to get to Greg.

The day at work seemed to drag. I desperately just wanted to get to the evening, to the drinks reception that Greg had invited me to, to see if I could pick up any further signals from him. Yesterday's lunch had started with so much promise and then he completely threw me by just wanting to talk about work and then telling me his wife was joining him. I couldn't figure him out and for some reason, I was obsessed with trying to. I wanted to know everything about him.

Although the day felt as though it had painstakingly ticked over, I was jubilant throughout. I thought I was funnier than normal, joining in with the other guy's banter and being overly helpful when Greg was in hearing distance. I didn't want him to take his eyes off me. I wanted him to look at me and want me like I wanted him. I was doing all of it for show and I was on good form, even if I do say so myself.

It was four o' clock and Greg gave me the nod that we had better think about leaving for the drinks reception then it occurred to me that in my mad dash to get out of the house this morning, I hadn't even asked Tom if I could be out late. I mean I hadn't told Tom I would be out late. *Shit.* My heart was racing with fear. He would go mad. *Write a quick text and then don't look at the phone again until the end of the evening.*

'Hey, sorry for the late notice. I have been asked to go to a drink's reception for work. It's a last minute thing as someone is ill. Sorry. Would've asked normally. Will be late back x'

I chucked my phone in my back hoping it would sink to the bottom of it like a stone being thrown into the sea, never to be found again. I was panicking. This is what he does to me. I can't cope with it anymore.

I went out to my car and brought in my bag of clothes to change into for the evening. I had packed a sophisticated yet sexy black number. It was very fitted and I had packed some additional jewellery to wear with it. I nipped into the ladies to get changed and emerged with my work clothes in a carrier bag. Everyone, as in every single one of them stopped what they were doing and looked at me. *Ok so now I feel self-conscious.* Feeling everyone's eyes on me, I slowly walked towards Greg's office. He looked up away from his screen and towards me, back to his screen and then immediately back to me. I didn't think the outfit was *that* special but it seemed to be having an effect. He looked flustered. I played it cool.

'Ready?'

'Yeah sure, I just need to send this email. You driving yeah? I'll leave my car here and get the train in tomorrow.'

'Yeah fine. See you at my car in a minute then.'

I tried to glide as I walked away from him. I had read about it in a magazine. It was an article about what makes French women so sexy. I had ticked off two of the requirements tonight – wear clothes a size too small and glide rather than walk. Well, I was trying to glide. *Don't trip, don't trip, don't trip.*

I made it out of the building and out to the car without stumbling. Part one of the mission accomplished. I leaned over to the glove box and pulled out 'Calvin Klein – Obsession' and doused myself in it. Less is not more when it comes to perfume. I want everyone to smell me tonight, particularly Greg. *Shit he's coming. Too late to check the rear mirror for lips, eyes and hair. He'll see me. Play it cool, play it cool.*

'Hey! Ready?'

'Fucking hell Kate. It smells like a brothel in here. Christ.' He started coughing and opened his window.

'My perfume. My car. My rules. You could always drive yourself Greg.'

'Alright you cheeky madam, let's go.'

As I drove us away he immediately began emailing on his phone. I had the radio on and so we barely spoke. I could feel his eyes on my legs. He was looking. I wasn't flashing anything. This was all him. He was pretending to be working but he was taking a good look.

'Leave your car at the venue tonight, I'll get you a taxi home. There will be champagne on arrival and you strike me as a girl who likes her bubbles.'

'You should never assume Greg. Do you know why? Because it makes an ASS out of U and ME. Get it?' I giggled at my reference to the company bullshit motivational posters that are dotted around the office.

'You are really quite goofy sometimes, do you know that? But you do like bubbles, don't you? I'm not wrong, am I?'

'I can be partial yes. Ok, you have twisted my arm. Let's get sozzled.'

We arrived at the venue and both separated to work the room but continuously catching each other's eye and smirking. A couple of times Greg beckoned me over to introduce me to a director of a law firm or a banker and each time handed me a fresh glass of champagne. The second time placing his hand on the small of my back making every hair stand up on end on my body. I laughed in the right places, acted demure where required, played the game to the best of my ability. We spent a couple of hours there and the room began to clear. I was hovering around pretending to listen to someone about agile and flexible working but the whole time watching Greg out of the peripheral of my eye. Waiting for my cue. I didn't know what the cue was but I was eager to find out what was going to happen next. He came over and introduced himself to my acquaintance and apologised on my behalf for being boring. My acquaintance corrected him and said that in actual fact he found me very charming and thought I would go far.

'Oh, without a doubt. Kate is one of the strongest in our team. She separates the men from the boys, this one. We just need to keep her feet on the ground sometimes, don't we Kate?' He looked at me and winked. My heart burst into a serious of flutters again. 'Anyway, we must get on. Lovely to meet you. Come on Kate, I promised not to keep you out late.' *Instant disappointment ensued.* We left the function room and Greg grabbed me and bustled me into the bar.

'What's going on?'

'I was bored shitless. Needed to get out of there. Drink?'

'Yes of course.'

We sat down at a table for two in the back corner. He had chosen it. He gestured for the waiter to come over like he owned the room.

'I'll have a pale ale and she will have a gin. Tanqueray with botanical soda, two cubes of ice and a wedge of lime.'

The waiter nodded and left a small serving of olives on the table.

'How do you know if I like gin?'

'I don't. I think you might and I think you will like the one I have ordered that's why I ordered it. No harm done if not, the next round is on you anyway.'

He oozed confidence and I liked it. He wouldn't be everyone's cup of tea but I think that's what made me like him more. I was happy for him to make decisions on my behalf and it was like looking in to what the future could look like. Quite often I felt like I was looking after Tom. It seemed to me that Tom had lost his way but Greg, Greg seemed to be a man who was very much in control. I also knew he would let me take the lead at times, it would be a balanced partnership.

'Shall we get something to eat? I'm starving.'

'Yeah sure, why not. Where are the menu's?'

'I don't mean here. God no. Plus, people I know might still be loitering and I don't want Chinese whispers starting. I'll get the bill and make a call.' He beckoned the waiter over and asked for the bill in some sort of sign language. Within five minutes he had booked us a table for two at an Italian around the corner, ordered a cab and paid the bill. I knew the Italian as I had been there on a date a few years back. It was very intimate. Tiny tables and dimly lit. I couldn't help but be assured that he was moving in on me. We could have just gone to a pub for something but this seemed like he was trying to make a good impression.

We arrived at Giuseppe's and were taken to our table. Greg took my jacket off and passed it to the waiter. He asked for the wine list and started scanning it. The waiter lit a candle for us and my heart was beating with how romantic this all felt. There were only a couple of tables with people dining and they were half way through their meals. We had arrived late I guess which made it seem all the more risqué to me.

'Do you like red?'

'Yes, Malbec usually.'

'Good taste. What would you say about this Argentinian?' He pointed to the list and the waiter kissed his fingers as a sign of a good choice.

'Great. A bottle of that please.'

Oh dear. I had already had two glasses of fizz, followed by two large gins and now he has ordered a bottle of wine. Work tomorrow could be a long day!

He started asking me questions. He wanted to know more about me. He wanted to know how things were with Tom. He told me I needed to get out of that relationship and said he was concerned with how controlling Tom was. I became quiet. *Was he just a concerned friend, caring boss?*

'Enough about me. I'll figure it out. I do need to end it, you're right. I just need to find the right moment. Anyway, so that I know what I am doing next time, why don't you tell me your secret? How does one find the right person and stay happily married for what, twenty years?'

'Don't ask me. I'm not happily married. I am painfully separating. Why else would I be sitting with a young, attractive woman in a discreet Italian restaurant at ten o' clock at night. That doesn't suggest a happy marriage, does it?'

I gulped. Then I picked up my wine and took a large sip and then looked at him as I placed the glass back on the table. It seemed like the room had got darker. It was either the wine haze or they had turned off some lights and left us only in the light of candles. This was becoming very seductive. The setting was completely right. The timing, however, wasn't.

'I'm sorry Greg, I didn't realise. I thought you were happy.'

'I am. Kind off. We are just figuring it all out. We should've split years ago but have tried for the kids. It just isn't working anymore. That's why she met me at that pub we were at... we can't talk at home with the kids there.'

'I see. So, you are separating then?'

'Yes, in a sense we already have. I have been living in the spare room for the last eighteen months.'

I suddenly felt a pang of joy followed by an immediate pang of shame. *Don't be happy for someone else's misery Kate.*

'Well, let's make a toast. To happier futures. It sounds like we both have shit to sort out.'

'I'll toast to that. Happier futures.' Our eyes were locked on each other. Something was happening. I refused to take my eyes away until he did but he didn't. We just held each other's stare both in the knowledge that we had no idea what the other person was thinking but we knew we were thinking about each other.

'Finish it with Tom, Kate. You need to. He's no good for you.'

The waiter interrupted our moment with our starters. I had ordered a mozzarella, tomato and basil salad and he had ordered prawns in chilli and garlic.

'Let's share. I like it that way.' He put both plates in the middle of the table and picked up a slice of the beef tomato from my plate. I didn't mind. In fact, I loved it. This felt very much like we were a couple yet he hadn't said that. I felt like he had been careful not to say anything but had wanted to. He had told me to end it with Tom. He told me his marriage was over. We were sharing food in an Italian restaurant late in the evening. Surely this meant something?

An hour or so later he was paying the bill and I was putting on my jacket. We had had a laugh. The wine had seen to that. He had been silly and I had enjoyed his entertainment. In between courses he had gone out for a cigar and I shared it with him, coughing and sputtering everywhere which he had found highly amusing. We had shared our main courses and we had talked. We talked and talked and talked. He asked questions and I asked questions. He laughed and I laughed. I forgot about where I was and what time of day it was. It felt as if I had been on holiday. Until we got into the taxi and I checked my phone. *Shit.*

'What's wrong?'

'It's Tom. He has called seventeen times and sent eight texts. He's angry. He says he has been to the hotel and knows I am not there. Fuck.' I was panicking. He was going to go mad when I got in. My face must've revealed my concerns.

'Don't worry! You have been out for dinner. You are allowed to eat, surely?'

'You don't know Tom.' Greg put his arm around me and pulled me in for a cuddle. I was terrified. What if he hits me this time. I have seen him get mad so many times before. He has punched walls, cupboards, whatever was nearest. Maybe this time it would be me.

'Don't worry. Tell him a group of us went out for dinner and I told you it would be a great networking opportunity. You will be fine but you need to realise that how you are feeling now is not normal Kate. The guy is bad news.'

We pulled up outside my flat and I thanked him for a lovely dinner. He smiled at me sympathetically which made me feel silly. He must think I am a complete wimp. I kissed him on the cheek and got out of the taxi and made my way into the block. *What the hell was I walking into.*

'Where the fuck have you been? I've called, sent loads of texts. Nothing!'

'Tom, I am sorry. A group of us went out for dinner. I did tell you I would be late.'

'Late? Late? Don't take the fucking piss Kate, where have you been and who the fuck with?' He was furious. His face was like a beetroot and I was scared. I tried to remain calm and not allow the situation to escalate.

'Tom, I haven't done anything wrong. I went for dinner. I told you I would be late. You are scaring me and so I am going to bed. I want you to sleep on the sofa.' He grabbed my face and slammed me against the wall.

'You fucking bitch!' He screamed in my face and his saliva sprayed on me. He was out of control.

'Tom. Let go of me. Now. This isn't ok.' He put his nose on mine.

'I should fucking teach you a lesson right now. You're nothing but a slut. This isn't finished Kate. This isn't fucking finished.' He pushed my head with his against the wall and then punched a hole in the wall next to my face.

'Look what you made me do! You are such a cunt! A fucking cunt!' He stormed through to the living room and slammed the door. I walked to our bedroom, shaking like a leaf and closed the door quietly. I got into bed with all my clothes on and lay there, shaking. I wasn't going to get much sleep tonight.

Chapter 9

I woke up with a startle. As soon as my eyes opened I wanted to know where he was and know that I was safe and in one piece. I looked around me and took in my familiar surroundings. I was relieved to know that I was at home and that I could see and hear normally and didn't appear to be in any form of pain. *Good, he didn't beat the shit out of me and I blacked out.* Call me dramatic but I was looking for wires taped up to me because I had been hospitalised. Once I had crossed that off I confirmed that I was not tied to the bed and that all my limbs were intact. As soon as I had accepted that I was safe and that he was not next to me, I jumped up and got ready for work as soon as I could, as quietly as I could. I didn't shower, I didn't want to awaken the beast. I threw on some clothes, tied my hair up, grabbed my make-up bag and darted. I popped my head around the living room door and there the ogre was. Sleeping, drooling. An empty bottle of red wine on the floor and a tumbler that would have had a whiskey in it. *Good* I thought. He must've knocked himself out with alcohol to absorb his guilt.

I arrived at work and stayed in the car to fix my hair and make-up. I was forty five minutes early. *Great. At least seeing Greg today will help my mood.* I picked up my phone and Greg had sent a text.

'Hey, I was worried about you last night but didn't want to text in case. I hope everything is ok. Call me anytime you need to talk. Not in your office today, back in London. G x' Mood deflates like a bouncy castle being taken down.

'Hey, everything is ok. Thanks. See you soon. K x'

I wanted to call him and tell him how scared I was, I knew I would probably cry and then he would realise how serious the situation was and he would come to my rescue. How he would come to my rescue I didn't know. What was he meant to do? Barge into my flat and physically remove Tom himself? That wasn't going to happen. He did ask me last night to end it with Tom. I don't know if that is because he knew I was in danger and he is worried or if because he wants me or both?

I made myself a coffee and sat down at my desk and began trawling through my emails but not really taking any of them in. Although my eyes were open and I was at work, all I could see was Tom pinning me against the wall. Phlegm spraying out of his purple face. *If looks could've killed...* Today is the day. Enough is enough. I cannot live my life like this anymore. I want a man like Greg. I know that is unlikely to be an option but what is certain is that I won't have a man like Greg all the while I am with Tom. I need to end it. If he kills me, he kills me. What's the alternative? I am going to end up dead at this rate anyway. I will send a text out, let my friends know that I plan to do it tonight and to check on me if they haven't heard from me by ten o'clock tonight. This is it. D day.

As I drove home from work I realised how quickly the day had gone and now I was almost at the point where I feared for my life. I had achieved quite a lot today. I had chased up all my outstanding quotes, made tea for everyone about four times, dialled out about forty times. It's amazing what you can get done when you don't want to think about your sad existence or think about the end of your existence. I pulled up in my reserved parking space at the back of the block. I hadn't thought about the perks of it before but in recent times, this space is where I would sit in my car trying to build up the courage to go into the flat not knowing which mood I was about to encounter. The space was out of view of any of my windows so I would sit there and collect my thoughts before going in and facing the Spanish Inquisition most nights. Who knew what I was walking into tonight but last night was pretty scary and I didn't plead for his forgiveness this time. He knows I'm changing. He knows he is losing me. *Here we go, time to rip off the plaster...*

I tentatively opened the door. I wasn't quiet. He needed to know I was here but I didn't call out to him either. I kicked off my shoes and put my handbag in the bedroom. *You can do this... you must do this.* I walked out of the room and saw him standing in the kitchen doorway smiling at me and holding flowers and a magazine. I walked towards him, took the gifts and placed them on the work top. I could see he had been cooking and it looked like one of my favourite meals. My heart sank. He knew what was coming.

'I bought you some magazines and flowers. There is wine in the fridge. I've made your favourite dinner. Is there anything else you want by way of an apology? Kate?' I held my head in my hands and took a deep breath.

'It's too late.' I slowly looked at him to make eye contact. He needed to know this was it.

'Kate...' he walked towards me, arms open. I walked back, arms closed.

'No. I'm sorry. It's over Tom.' A tear rolled down my cheek and I backed out of the kitchen and went into the living room and slowly began to pace.

'Kate, babe, I am sorry. I lost control. I'm sorry. It won't happen again. Please.'

'No. Sorry. This is it.' I couldn't look at him.

'What? That's it? I make one mistake and that's it? For fuck sake Kate.' *Here we go... Irrational explosion imminent...*

'It hasn't been one mistake Tom and you know it. I've made up my mind and I'm sorry but I cannot do this anymore. You scare me! I am scared of you. That is not ok.'

'Oh, shut up. Scared of me? Like you are so fucking perfect. Do you know how much shit I put up with from you? No normal guy would take your treatment lying down. You need reminding who is the man sometimes. Swanning about on your corporate do's. You can be a complete bitch Kate. You are lucky to have me. You know you won't find another me. You know I will be snapped up in no time unlike you. You will be here on your own for a long time with your cat like the sad bitch that you are.'

'Tom, I am not doing this. I am not "hashing this out". We are over. As of now and I need you to leave. Please find somewhere to stay and make arrangements to come back for the rest of your stuff. I want you gone tonight.'

'Kate come on. Stop being a bitch.' He was pacing. I was getting more afraid but I knew the end was in sight. I stayed silent.

'Ok fuck you. I will go but you'll be sorry.' He left the living room. He was gone for all of ten minutes before he emerged with a duffle bag. I stood up to see him out. He grabbed me and slammed me down on the sofa, gripping my face.

'I'll go you fucking bitch but if I find out this is about someone else I will finish you and him you fucking whore. I did everything for you. Everything. And this is how you treat me? You deserve nothing you fucking bitch. You will regret this. Mark my words you slut, you will regret this.' He pushed me deep into the sofa and stepped back. He was staring at me, breathing heavily as the blood slowly drained from his furious face. My heart was racing. Then he left. I sat on the floor with my head in my hands and cried. I wasn't crying because I was sad. They were tears of relief.

Then he was back. *Why the fuck didn't I lock the door!* I sprang to my feet and wiped my tears. He came in and looked at me and then gently took my face.

'Look at you. See, you don't want this. What is this about? I decided to come back in case you changed your mind and wanted to talk and I can see now that you have.' I saw the keys on the side and grabbed them.

'I haven't changed my mind. Nothing has changed. Leave and don't come back. Only for your things. By appointment.'

'Are you fucking kidding me?' I opened the balcony doors and stepped outside.

'Get the fuck out. Leave now and don't fucking touch me. You are a bastard and I want nothing to do with you. Get out.' I shouted loudly but not too loud. Enough to scare him into wondering who might have heard. He pointed his finger at me and said nothing. He shook his head and left. I waited until I saw him outside the block and then I ran to the door and double locked it and put the safety chain on. Relief.

I went to the fridge and poured myself a large glass of wine. My phone was staring at me from the work top. All I wanted to do was call Greg but I couldn't. It didn't seem right. However, as though he was reading my mind, Greg had texted me.

'How are you? Everything ok? Hope it's ok to text. G xx' *Fuck it, I'm phoning him.*

'Hello? You ok?'

'Yeah I'm fine. I hope you don't mind me calling?'

'Not at all. How is everything?'

'I've done it. I have ended it.'

'What! Wow. I wasn't expecting that. Well, this calls for a celebration and I think I should be the one to take you out.' I laughed half-heartedly. This wasn't feeling as good as I was hoping it would. Once again, Greg wasn't giving me the medicine I wanted, he was just giving me a wet paper towel. I didn't have anything to say as the reality of my situation began to kick in.

'Shit. Sorry, that was insensitive. I didn't mean to say celebrate. I meant you need to take your mind off things and I will gladly take you out for a drink when you are ready. That's what friends are for.' *Friends? Friends! I don't want any more fucking friends. I want my wounds to be licked.*

'That would be lovely.'

'Listen Kate, I've got to go. I've just got home. We'll speak soon. Bye.' Before I even got a chance to say anything else he had hung up. I necked my glass of wine, curled up in a ball on my bed and let the tears roll out.

Chapter 10

The next couple of days passed by in a hungover haze of disappointment. The good thing about kicking out your fiancé on a Thursday means you have the whole weekend to numb any emotion out with alcohol. We all know it doesn't work really. It only helps to pass the evening and to secure you a place in the land of slumber. It also secures a place in emotional hell the next day as the hangover depression and anxiety kicks in making you think that you are in a worse place than you actually are. It's not surprising that even the strongest of people can become alcoholics. It's a vicious circle and a treacherous path to go down if you enter it in a vulnerable state. Using alcohol to quieten the evil inner dialogue and then needing it the following day to cure the headache and all-round feeling of shittiness is not a smart way.

I made a pact with myself. I gave myself permission to get obliterated on booze for this weekend and this weekend only as a coping mechanism. I knew the stages of grief and I wanted to deal with them as quickly as possible. I knew that ending it with Tom was the right thing to do but it didn't mean I could avoid the feeling of loss. The time that I had invested going to waste. The dreams that amounted to nothing. The picture of my future taken down from the wall of hope and put on the bonfire of reality. That hurt. A lot of it hurt. I wanted to be in love and I wanted to be loved back. I wanted someone to adore me. Not someone to suck me in and then try and imprison me and change all the things that made them fall in love with me. Why could none of the men I had dated so far remain who they were in the beginning? Why did they always have to convert to the religion of controlling and possessive behaviour? What was I doing to contribute to this? Was there something about a guy that I would always go for but couldn't see? I had to take responsibility for my part in this. I had to learn in order to prevent it from happening again. I knew I must learn something from these continued failed relationships but I just couldn't see where I was going wrong.

Over the break-up weekend I ignored my phone. I didn't want to speak to my friends. I wanted to get sad, get drunk, play love songs, have a cry and get it out of my system. I knew it would only be a matter of time before I was back on track and feeling full of life again. A feeling I hadn't had for the last eighteen months. It seemed like I would be feeling footloose and fancy free quicker than expected.

I broke up with Tom on Thursday evening. I had three glasses of wine and no dinner resulting in a fairly successful attempt at getting to sleep easily. On Friday, I was glad to go to work and be distracted by the office buzz for the day. I was also glad that Greg was not around. I wanted him to see me on form. I did not want him to see me vulnerable and putting a brave face on things. No one else would be able to tell I was vulnerable but I had a feeling that he would. I knew the power he had over me and I had to at least try to keep some of my strength and wits about me. He was dangerous territory and I knew it. If he was going to suck me in it would be when I was strong enough to see him for who he was, not vulnerable enough to cling on to whatever game he offered. To the outsiders, I breezed through the day making lots of sales calls, chasing up deals and offering hot drinks to my colleagues more than I needed to. To them I was on good form, to me I was masking my life falling apart.

When I got home that evening I was numb. The house was empty of life and so was I. I knew I had made the right choice and yet I didn't feel as sad or as happy as I expected to. Just numb. I got undressed as normal. I had a shower as normal. I pulled on my comfortable jogging bottoms and a loose t-shirt. The clothes matched what I needed out of life. No pressure and no restrictions. I went to the fridge and got some wine out. I poured it into a glass and watched as it's ice cold temperature steamed up the glass I had just rinsed and towel dried. I caught myself staring at it, transfixed by it. I put both hands on the worktop, looked up with my eyes closed and inhaled deeply. I didn't feel anything, just completely flat. I knew this meant that the emotion was coming but not right now. If it wasn't coming I would be happier. The fact that I was so flat meant that a crash was definitely coming my way.

The balcony was calling me and I thought it would be better to be flat and redundant behind my shades, sitting in the sun than just staring into space in the kitchen. *Better take the bottle out with me.*

The evening passed and I had barely moved. I had some secret cigarettes although they weren't much of a secret as I wasn't hiding from anyone and I drank most of the wine over the course of three hours. I had given everything thought apart from my situation. I thought about how long the trees that I could see had been planted for and how long it would take for them to be higher than the nearby houses. They would've been planted when these flats were built five years ago. I wondered who got to decide what trees to plant and where. *Surely there must be some sort of risk assessment for this kind of job. In this day and age, you can't just plant a tree anywhere without pissing someone off, surely? What a fucking mundane job. Actually, sounds alright. If that's the height of the stress, it's not too bad actually.* The train of thought then ran off to what this person might look like and how did they end up becoming Chief Tree Planter. I've always thought it's weird how some people just fall into odd jobs. Surely no one at school decides that they want to be in charge of where trees go on new housing estates. That is just a snippet as to what went through my head on that balcony. There was a lot of stuff to look at and I was out there for a while so you get the idea. It wasn't until I needed a wee and had to remove myself from the seat that I had pretty much melted into that I realised I hadn't spared a thought for Tom or Greg. That made me happy. I was doing ok. I was tipsy but I was doing ok.

I glided through the house like a spirit looking for its body. It's as if I wasn't present. I was just going through the motions. I put the small remainder of wine back in the fridge and poured a pint of water. Consuming all of that in one go to prevent a headache tomorrow and then filling up the glass again to take to bed, I lazily and broken heartedly skimmed my feet along the floor through to my bedroom. I don't think the decision had been mine. It was as if my body took me. It's as if there was another me that was looking after broken me and knew that what I needed was to lie down.

Now on the bed fully clothed, I lay on my left side and faced the wall and stared into space. Nothing was going through my mind. Not a thing. All I could hear was my breathing, that was all I had for company. That and a feeling as though something had been removed from me. A love lobotomy. I thought about playing some music but that meant looking at my phone and so I chose to remain in my silent stupor.

I woke up to an unwelcome racket being made by some crows outside. I hadn't closed the curtains when I lay down last night and as such, I was now awake at 6.30am. As soon as I woke I was wobbly. Today was the day. Breakdown imminent. I knew it was coming and it wasn't that far away so, in an attempt to defeat it I decided to get up and seize the day at this ridiculous hour. I would never normally be seen up at this time on a Saturday unless I was going on holiday but desperate times called for desperate measures as the old adage would have us believe. I had escaped a fuzzy head. I couldn't help but feel that was the God's offering me a trade. 'We will remove any chance of a hangover but it is going to be replaced with emotional turmoil. Good luck!'

Like a zombie and on autopilot, I carried myself through to the kitchen to make my morning lemon water and a coffee. I still seemed to be gliding. I filled the kettle and caught myself looking out of the window at nothing in particular. If anyone looked in I would look like a mad woman especially with my sleep crafted Bonnie Tyler hairdo. Back in the 80's this was a strong look but if I went to the shop now I would expect someone to take me by the elbow and ask me if everything was alright. My chin started to wobble and that was my cue to stop daydreaming and put the kettle on.

As I waited for my hot drinks to cool, I got myself into the shower. After a night of Sauvignon Blanc and too many cigarettes, I needed to clean up straight away. My mouth was like a rat had died in it and that wasn't helping my already fragile mood. I couldn't be arsed if I was honest but I knew I had to at least attempt to have a normal day. I stepped in and after standing there for a couple of minutes staring into space I got the shower gel and began trying to cleanse my body hoping it would massage its way into my soul. Something didn't feel right. Something was out of place and it took me far longer than it should've done to figure it out. I was washing my bra in circular motions with shower gel. I hadn't taken it off when I got in. I had managed to remove everything else, every single other item of clothing but somehow, I missed my bra. I unclipped it and dropped it on the floor and let out a slight snigger. I guess that's what I get for having not eaten a morsel yesterday and then having three quarters of a bottle of wine.

I would get my act together today. Shower, clean my teeth, have my coffee and then head out somewhere. The key to heartache is to keep busy. I remember the rules from last time when I said I wouldn't do this again. I would like to tell you now that I won't do this again but we all know that's not a promise I will keep.

Once dressed I sat down at the dining table with my coffee and looked at my phone. I had several unread messages from Tom.

I deliberate whether it's a good idea to read them or not but I also know there is no point in putting it off if I want to move on and so with a deep breath I open them. The first is nice... kind of. He says he didn't want this and he wished we could put the clock back. The next says he loves me and misses me. The third asks where I am and why am I not replying. The fourth says that if I am out fucking someone else already he will find out and he will kiss us both. The fifth is a list of names he calls me and is just pure vitriol and at that point I delete his whole thread of messages and block his number. I can see where it is going and it won't be pretty and I don't want to hear it. There is no point in talking to him when I don't want to fix anything so best just to block him and move on.

Tears. They come and they are flowing fast. This is what I was waiting for and I knew it was coming. I allow myself to cry. I know I have to get it out of my system. I cry at the table and although I am hurting I am surprised by how I am not sobbing. Just crying. I've been worse and that fills me with some hope that this recovery won't take too long. Then I get a text and it's from Greg;

'Hey good looking, how are you feeling? Xxx'

'Not great. A bit upset but I'll be ok. You? Xx'

'Upset? Why?' I note that he hasn't put any kisses and wonder if that was deliberate or just a quick reply.

'Umm, because I have split up from my fiancé. I know it was the right thing to do but I still feel sad. Xx' He doesn't text back and my instinct tells me that he is annoyed about me having any feelings. Typical bloke. I am sad about the end, the unfulfilled dreams and promises, the wasted time and energy, the change in a person, the closing of the chapter. I am not sad to lose Tom. I just feel empty but Greg doesn't get that. And how could he by a text?

I am now saddened by the fact that I have another man who wants it all to be about him in my life and so I take myself over to the sofa and lie down on it and begin my second session of crying. For a brief moment, the tears subside and I maximise that slot to go and draw the curtains and surrender myself to the day of misery ahead. I get out my Sex and The City box set and look at my watch, *too early for wine*, and curl up on the sofa.

After two episodes, I am feeling better and am glad that I have been blubbing. I feel more rational for it. I get up realising it is now approaching midday and in my rule book, that means a glass of wine is acceptable on a Saturday at this hour. I pick up my phone and see that Greg has text again and I instantly feel happier.

'You've got nothing to feel bad about. There are far better men out there and you are closer to having the right one now. Chin up and let's go for that drink soon xxx' *Hmmm back to three kisses.*

I walk to the kitchen with a definite spring in my step. My interpretation of that text is that he thinks he is the better man and that I am going to have him and suddenly the sun is shining and the crows crowing don't sound so harsh after all. I even open the curtains again.

Chapter 11

My plans to be by myself and be miserable for the next forty-eight hours were scuppered by my friends Katya and Gerrard. One of my favourite couple friends. Katya used to be a lesbian, well, she still was but through Gerrard she found out she could love a man too. She even married a girl once and they seemed happy for a good couple of years or so. No one knows how it all came about but from what I gather she came home from work one night, found her wife sitting on the sofa in nothing but her pants and an old t-shirt and saw a tampon cord hanging out and felt physically repulsed. She kicked her out, we all went clubbing a few times and then Gerrard appeared. Katya tried to tell us for ages that they were just friends but we all knew she had turned to the penis side. She gradually morphed into a heterosexual and swapped hoodies for dresses and trainers for heels. Not that I am stereotyping, that's just the way it went and she's never seemed happier.

Who knows, I might try it myself one day. Go lesbian I mean. Not. I can't deal with my own hormones let alone someone else's. Lesbians are brave if you ask me. As are the gays. Lesbians face 'body synching' each month and having a double dose of PMT which can't be fun and as for the gays, well, they have to fight over the mirror continually and compete over who's the funniest or the most outrageously bitchiest. That's how it seems to be with my friends anyway. I seem to have a lot of gay friends. I love them. They never fail to make me smile and trust me, a gay will never let you be sad alone. They can't guarantee your happiness but they can guarantee you a bloody good party and to cry with you at three in the morning whilst all singing Purple Rain into hairbrushes. Katya claimed not to be gay anymore but she will always be gay to me.

Katya had sent a text advising me of her and Gerrard's plans for a barbeque that afternoon and said if I was around, my attendance was required. I was also invited to bring Tom. I replied telling her that Tom was no more and to which she replied telling me that it was no longer an invitation and more of a demand. 'Bring booze and PJ's xxxx' she said was all that was required. The text came at a good time, actually. The sun was shining and Greg's text had given me hope that there would be more to life than just me and my cat. I don't have a cat yet but it's inevitable at this rate.

I got myself ready and grabbed my toothbrush and PJ's. That was all that was obligatory apart from stopping en-route to purchase PARTAY essentials. I have never been one for hanging around the next day. I prefer to get home and get back to normality and shift the hangover as quickly as possible and I can't do that if I am not in my own surroundings.

We are starting early at Katya's and although that should dictate an early evening, it won't. She will end up pulling out a secret bottle of alcohol when we are starting to flag and call shots to everyone. We will all get a second wind and party into the early hours. That means I need to arrive well equipped. I stop off and grab a four pack of ciders (essential summer drink to be served with ice), bottle of white wine (to chill whilst we have a cider) to be sipped graciously and then for the floor filler, a party classic, the friend that everyone likes, a bottle of spiced rum, a bottle of coke and a bag of limes to go with. I throw a bag of sharing crisps into the basket as well just so that the cashier can see we are sophisticated drinkers and realise on the way out that the bag of crisps makes it look like there is a bigger problem than there is. Next time I might swap the crisps for paracetamol and give them something to talk about.

Why is it at the grand old age of twenty seven, I feel paranoid about buying a basket of booze? In my early twenties, I would have seen it as something to be proud of but everyone knows young twenty somethings party all the time. When you're heading for thirty and above it looks like there is a problem. There is, I suppose. I have just called off my wedding and cancelled plans to be Cara's stepmother. That makes me feel sad. *It was the right thing to do.* I reassure myself and look at my bag of booze and tell myself that Captain Morgan will counsel me this weekend along with my lovely friends. I have enough booze to take us all into the early hours and ensure that we all have a deep sleep. Sunday will be a write off and I can spend it lounging on the sofa whilst watching a film and prepare myself for a new week and a fresh, single, start.

I arrive at Katya's at around the same time as our other friend, Ryan. He is a big gay ball of energy and has just returned from a trip to Dubai with his hairstylist boyfriend. They were the epitome of fun and whenever they went away they came back with the most ludicrous stories of what they got up to. Somehow, they always managed to party with a backing dancer or a make-up artist or a C list celebrity's cousin.

Ryan came bounding in through the door wearing a baseball cap, muscle vest and ripped jeans and looks like he had been to America, not the middle east. He has had the time of his life evidently and tells us all about the friends they made and how enriching the experience was. I love him.

Katya is busy making cocktails and I fill Ryan in on the Tom and Greg saga. He is delighted that Tom has been given the heave ho. He has hated him for a long time and was the first one to see through his fake demeanour. He had been urging me to walk for some time but admitted he didn't think I ever would. I tell him about Greg and instantly he tells me going to a man that is married (separated) will be a big mistake. He says I could do without the baggage and I think he is just scared he will be another Tom. As if by magic he sends a text and asks what I am up to with a couple of kisses. Ryan grabs my phone, pulls me in for a selfie showing off our glasses of prosecco that he brought and we both do cheesy grins. He replies to Greg;

'Having fun with my bestie, what about you? Xx' and he hits send before I can say boo to a goose.

'I thought you didn't approve?' I enquire and take my phone back.

'I don't but the prosecco does!' and he grabs the bottle and fills up my glass.

The afternoon doesn't slow down and we all become boozy and the general consensus is that everyone is delighted that I have broken up with Tom. They tell me now that they all thought he was a wanker but they didn't want to say anything every time I complained about him (which I did a lot) because although they knew there were problems, they all thought I would stick with him, forever. I look at my life from the outside in and think how sad and pathetic I must've seemed. I don't think about it for that long though, the constant pouring of drinks and offerings of nibbles see to that plus we all have loads to catch up on and as a group of typical tipsy twenty something's, we are all fighting to get a word in.

I go to check my phone not expecting anything but I am surprised to find four texts from Greg. The first is a picture message of him and his mate. They are in a pub somewhere. The second one says, 'Great minds think alike xxx', the third says 'Would rather be at your party though xxx' and the fourth says 'Hope you're ok xxxx'

I show Ryan out of earshot of Katya and Gerrard. I can't see them approving of me jumping out of the frying pan into the fire, they would just worry about me. Ryan becomes very excitable and tells me that he wants me. I send him a sweet but generic reply and he instantly replies.

This goes on for the next few hours. He wants more pictures and constant updates. He says he wants some pictures of me to show his friend. A bit of an odd request but after doing a quick recce we discover he isn't on Facebook and decide that this is a fair request. We are also extremely tipsy, if not drunk, and are both enjoying the chase and banter with Greg. I think Ryan is just desperate to make sure I don't get back with Tom, having been disappointed when I took him back last time.

As expected, Katya serves up a big, delicious and much needed chilli with rice and pitta breads to soak up the afternoon shenanigans. I think we are glad of the break from the booze and the sun and the noise level reduces and we become less animated. The booze break lasts for all of half an hour when the table is being cleared and drinks are being suggested again. I go to the kitchen and knock back a pint of water, hoping but knowing that it won't prevent a hangover tomorrow and use the opportunity to check my phone again. More texts from Greg. I smile from the bottom of my tummy. It literally feels like my insides are full of joy.

The evening proceeds and as expected there is lots of tomfoolery, dancing, singing, shots and general high-jinx and good times. It's about three am and we are about to call it a night. I suggest to Ryan that maybe I could invite Greg over tomorrow. He tells me to go for it but he is drunk. I have slowly sobered up and have been drinking water when no one has been watching. The hard party goers would not approve of water between drinks. I however, do not approve of feeling like shit tomorrow and knowing my emotions are not in a sound place right now. My theory, however, is that I could text Greg now and invite him over tomorrow. When he says no, I can tell him that I was drunk and that I am very sorry and that it won't happen again knowing full well that I wasn't drunk, knew exactly what I was doing and knew exactly what I was after.

'Had a very boozy but very fun night. Off to bed now. Was thinking you could pop round to mine tomorrow if you fancy it. Night K Xxx'

I went to bed and hadn't noticed that he replied instantly;

'I would love that. G xxxx'

Chapter 12

The next morning, I woke up earlier than I would've liked. I was bunked up with Ryan on a mattress on the spare room floor surrounded by Katya's photography projects. My mouth was worse than an ill-treated and over-worn flip flop and I could tell that I was over the limit to drive so would be here for a little longer. Ryan was fast asleep. Not for much longer, if Kate's awake, everyone is awake.

'Oi.' I give him a nudge. 'Wake up.' Deep sighs follow by some form of tribal cave grunts.

'What time is it?'

'I don't know, I left my phone downstairs. I think Katya and Gerrard are having sex. Listen.'

'What the fuck is wrong with you Kate. You woke me up to listen to our recently turned straight friend having sex with her new boyfriend. That is not something I need to hear right now. Men and women having sex repulses me.' He leans over anyway and picks his phone up off the floor. 'For fuck sake Kate, it's 6.45am.' He makes a false crying noise.

'Sorry, couldn't get back to sleep and wanted your company. I can hardly go and make a coffee with that slapping going on, can I? I don't want to hear it either and I knew you would feel the same so I thought we would be better in it together.'

'Thanks for thinking of me. Oh well, you got what you wanted. I'm awake. Now what?'

'We wait for them to stop having it off and I will go and make you an apologetic coffee.'

'That's a good starting point. What a night. What time did we go to bed? My head is pounding, I think I'm still pissed.'

'Even if you're not, you look like you are because your eyeliner is all over your face and you look like you could be in the video for 'Let me entertain you' by Robbie.'

'Cheers for that babe. Oh god they really are having sex. How does that work at this hour of the day? I never thought Katya would be a moaner. Is this awkward?'

'No because she is our friend. We all have sex so we just have to grin and bear it. It can't go on for much longer.'

'I don't know Kate, it's hangover sex. If my new found love / hangover sex is anything to go by we could be trapped in here all day. I know I wouldn't let Gerrard get off lightly. He could have my pork sword any time he wants it. Just go and make a coffee. That will make them stop.'

'Ok, I will but how about when we leave here today you come back to mine. I will do us a Sunday roast. I am too fragile to face this hangover alone.'

'Yeah ok it's a deal. Now go and make me a coffee.'

'Great. DON'T go back to sleep.'

I peel my alcohol abused body off the bed and stand up. The room spins slightly and what should have been an effortless movement has caused me to break into a sweat and pause in case I am sick. I take a few deep breaths and decide I am safe to move again. I open the door loudly enough and offer a little splutter to let our lovers know we are awake and delicately make my way down the stairs, breathing out a deep sigh with each step on the way down.

As I make the coffee I spot my phone on the side and all of a sudden last night comes flooding back with horror. God knows how many times I had texted Greg but it was lots. He was texting back but still, if my boozy memory serves me right the messages took a turn away from professional, away from friendship even and bombed along the horny lover's bypass. I should not be allowed my phone after three drinks. I need to implement that rule immediately. Any time there is a party, everyone puts their phones in the bowl at the beginning. Similar, but not to be confused with, putting keys in a bowl but which much safer consequences.

'Shit! I invited him over!' Suddenly I felt sick as I stirred the two, strong black coffees. *Why oh why did I think that would be a good idea.* I want to cry as I gingerly make my way up the stairs with the two coffees.

I kick the door open with my foot and Ryan is sleeping.

'Oi. Cinderella. Wake up.' Cue similar grunting noises to fifteen minutes ago. 'I need your help. I have fucked up big time.' This gets an instant reaction and he sits up, chomping at the bit to hear what I've done. 'The last message I sent Greg last night, well this morning, was inviting him over to mine today.'

'Oh, you twat.'

'I know, I know.'

'He's your boss. You are only just single. Don't shit on your own doorstep. Right now, you need your job. It's all you have.'

'Alright Einstein. I am fully aware that I have done something stupid. I need you to help me get out of it. Can I say you stole my phone and you wrote it?'

'Is he five? In which case, he might believe that. Nope, you're going to have to tell him you were drunk and it was a silly idea but he is a man and he knows now that you want him and so he will find a way to get in your knickers. Because, you've made it obvious that's what you want.'

We both lean back with our coffees and sigh.

'Fuck cooking a roast. We'll get a Chinese and watch Dirty Dancing.' We both clink our coffees and sigh, again.

About an hour had passed and another coffee had been consumed along with a pint of water and I was ready to go home. I desperately needed to get out of my clothes, get showered and scrub my teeth. It was impossible to know how hungover I was until I had completed my ablutions. Only then, could the damage be fairly assessed. I grabbed my few belongings and picked up my phone of which the battery was dead. I was glad about that and was scared to see whatever drunken humiliation I had inflicted on today by looking at last night's evidence so the phone could stay turned off as far as I was concerned.

Katya and Gerrard had gone to sleep and Ryan was probably going to doze off as well. I said goodbye to him and told him to pass on my love to the other two.

'Text me when you get back babe and we will sort out a time for later.'

'Will do.' I leaned in for the obligatory departing cuddle, both of us avoiding breathing on each other.

I get into my car and realise I am probably still a tiny bit over the limit but I am desperate to get home so I will just take it easy. I only have a few miles to go. I drive back on autopilot, replaying last night's events, conversations, tomfoolery, text messages over and over. I realise I am smiling broadly. Whatever happens with Greg, and hopefully I haven't made a tit out of myself, I know I can and will be happy. There are lots of bachelors out there. My boss is probably the one I should stay furthest away from but texting him last night reassured me about my decision with Tom and I knew I was going to be ok. If anything, I couldn't believe how quickly I was recovering from Tom. I was glad that it didn't seem to knock me that much but I was confused how I could've ever been engaged to someone who it was so easy to leave. *He was a complete arse Kate. You were only with him for that long because you were scared to leave.*

As I pulled up outside the flat I felt a surge of elation at how free I was. I hadn't been this free in years. I was coming home having partied with friends all night, I had the day ahead of me and had invited my friend over for dinner, I was free to text and speak to whoever I wanted and I could dress how I wanted. All of these things without having to ask or answer to anyone. Suddenly I felt alive. It was as if in that moment that the clouds shifted to let the sun beam down on me and I pretty much skipped into the block of flats.

I let myself in and poured another water, put my phone on charge and stripped before jumping in the shower. I came out feeling brand new. You cannot beat washing off a hangover. Getting the cigarette smoke out of your hair, the film of filth out of your mouth. I let out a groan of satisfaction after spitting out my toothpaste and dabbed my face dry with the hand towel. Today was going to be a good day, I could just feel it!

I sat down on the edge of the bed in my towel and took a minute. Although, I was feeling good I hadn't been let off completely scott-free. The heat of the shower and the hangover sweats made me feel a bit dizzy so I just needed to take it easy. *Oh I said I would text Ryan! Four messages?*

First message is Katya. She says I am a twat for driving home and must've been over the limit. She doesn't know that I swapped my shot glass for hers several times last night so she had twice as many as me.

Second text is Ryan. 'Did you get home ok? I'm just having a coffee with Katya and will then head to yours. Ok to shower at yours?'

'Home safely, sorry had to charge my phone. Come over whenever xx'

Third text is Greg. I can hardly bare to open it when I realise he has sent two messages. I really want to ignore it but I can't, so with my stomach in knots, I open it with one eye...

'I would love that. G xxxx' I wasn't expecting that but he sent it at 3.03am and so the next text will be him saying that it was a silly idea and he's not coming. I slowly scroll down...

'What's your postcode and what time? I need to juggle a few things around here but could probably get to you for around 1pm? Xxx' Sent at 8.36am today.

'Holy shit.' I stand up and begin pacing the room immediately. I am a complete fifty-fifty mix of excitement and sickening nerves. Like with all good opportunities that come to me, doubt creeps in and I immediately start thinking of reasons to back out knowing that this is too good for me and I don't feel worthy. *Phone Ryan, he will know what to do.*

I didn't get what I had hoped for from Ryan. He wants to see what will happen and appears to be enjoying the mess that I have created. I tried to get him to come over anyway so that it wouldn't be weird and we could all just have a coffee together but he refused 'to be piggy in the middle' and has now backed out completely. He also confirmed my fear that I cannot cancel Greg because he is my boss and I don't want to piss him off. He has made it clear he wants to come over and so I am going to have to roll with it. Anyway, nothing has to happen. We are just two friends who happen to be catching up on a Sunday. Two recently separated friends who were texting until the early hours of this morning, who swapped photo messages of each other... *Nothing needs to happen.*

Chapter 13

I pace the living room wondering what the hell I am getting myself into. Everyone knows that the best way to get over one man is *not* to get under another. The temporary fix creates a longer-term problem. But, he is my boss. I can't just cancel on him now. He will see it as me messing him about and then he will sack me. I will just have to run with it. Perhaps if I pretend to be really hungover, maybe make up some disgusting habit that he doesn't know about, dumb myself down a bit, he might go off me. That could work! Make myself less appealing.

'Fuck. He is here.' I watch him pull up in his very expensive and quite sexy looking sports car. 'No backing out now' I say to myself in disbelief that this is happening. The saliva is building in my mouth and I feel somewhat perspired.

I watch him out of my kitchen window on the first floor. I can see him but he can't see me. He looks calm. He looks completely at ease. Not like me. I am a nervous wreck. He just looks like a normal guy walking along the pavement without a care in the world. The buzzer rings. A hurried glance in the mirror, a quick patting down of the hair and it's show time. How I wish it wasn't show time and that I was just curled up on the sofa with a chick flick, festering in my own misery but with job security. I pick up the phone to let him in to the building.

I am actually hyperventilating. I am shaking. I am terrified. This is ridiculous. *Nothing needs to happen, Kate.*

I open the door, smile, say hi and step back immediately so he can't lean in for a kiss. I start rambling and walk through the flat, leading the way. I offer him a beer without really listening to his response of how he is today. He denies the beer and asks for coffee. *Shit, I really fancied a hair of the dog.*

'Sure, I can do coffee. Let's go for the posh stuff.' Bizarrely, I feel good about having filter coffee in and subtly push the Kenco jar out of view. He strikes me as someone who would not approve of instant coffee.

'So, how's the head Ms Roberts? Sounds like you hit it hard last night.'

'Oh god, do you know I haven't even looked at my phone. I saw your message about coming over but I haven't gone back further as I'm sure I embarrassed myself and right now "the head" is too fragile to face it.'

'You have nothing to be embarrassed about. It was nice. I enjoyed the messages.'

My heart is racing and I decide it's time for diversion tactics. I hand him his coffee whilst quickly looking at him up and down and taking him in. He's wearing cream chinos and a Ralph Lauren shirt. His trademark couple of buttons are undone around the neck allowing me just a small peek at his chest hair and I find my mind wandering once more. I smile at him and make my way through to the living room. I sit down in a corner of my L shaped sofa and am relieved that he takes the other corner. My hand that is holding the coffee mug is shaking violently. I don't know if it's the hangover shakes or nerves. In fact, I think it is a terrible case of both. I put my cup down without trying to spill it.

'You ok there, Roberts? You appear to have the shakes.'

'I wasn't holding it properly and it was burning my knuckle.'

'Oh right. And there was me thinking you were nervous.'

'Nervous? Oh, he's a confident one. What is there to be nervous about? We are just two friends having a coffee.'

He picks up his coffee and takes a sip. All is silent but oddly, it's not awkward. It's fairly obvious we are both thinking. Thinking very loudly.

'So, have you heard from Tom?' And relax. We are now in the folds of generic chit chat. Safe territory. I fill him in on Tom and tell him about the previous night's antics with my friends and about Ryan and I hearing Katya and Gerrard having it off this morning. We end up in fits of giggles. I notice I have told him detail, I have given him an account of what I have been doing and he hasn't given anything back. He just shows a lot of interest in me and makes lots of quick witted jokes about the information I have offered. I decide not to push him. He will talk about his separation when he is ready. I asked him how he was and how things are so it's not like I didn't try. He must not want to share yet and that's fine. I am happy to fill in the gaps.

Having finished our coffee's, I pick up the cups and ask him if he wants another.

'No thanks, I don't have time. I need to make a move in a minute.' Suddenly I feel deflated and wish he could stay. Crazy. An hour ago, I was desperate to cancel and now I don't want him to leave.

'Ok that's cool. I suppose I should get on too. You know, get back to my hangover. Thanks for popping round though. It was nice. We should do it again.' He is staring at me and my heart begins to race. Something is brewing.

'Kate? Why am I here?'

Fuck. Oh shit, oh shit, oh shit. Is this a trick question?

'What? For a coffee? As I said, we are just two friends having a coffee.'

'Is that all it is for you?'

I break out into a sweat. I honestly don't know what the right thing is to say. I begin to splutter.

'Kate. The more time I spend with you... the more I realise...'

'Realise what?'

Fuck he is going to sack me. He has come round to tell me we have crossed boundaries and he can't have me in the office anymore. I do not need this right now.

'I realise that I am falling in love with you.'

Mind blown. I was not expecting that and I am lost for words. I realise I need to reply.

'Wow. I wasn't expecting that. I thought you were about to sack me.'

He starts to laugh.

'Sack you? No way. You are one of the best sales people we have. Plus, I like having you around. So, do you like me?'

'I would've thought that was fairly obvious, Greg. Yes, I do and I have done for some time but we were both… well, you know what we were and we work together. It's not ideal.'

'I'm moving. I have been offered a promotion and agreed it with the board last week but that is top secret. I am going to be heading up the European offices and will be travelling a lot. Don't say a word. No announcement will be made for a few months.'

I'm quietly disappointed that I won't be seeing him popping into the office as regularly. It must show on my face. He takes my chin and looks at me straight on.

'Hey, this is a good thing. I could never start a relationship with you whilst we worked together. I am leaving the UK branches and now we can be together. I just have a few loose ends to tie up as you know. Whilst I do that, I think we should start spending some time together and get to know each other better. I will move out soon and once I have done that, we can go public. I just need a few months, is that ok?'

I cannot believe my ears. The UK Sales Director of the business, the successful, witty, charming, funny, gorgeous Greg Owen wants me! He makes all my exes look like mice. He is a real man. He is a grown up. He is established. He is a gentleman. He cares about me and he wants me.

'Of course that's ok. I would like that very much. Let's take our time.'

He smiles at me, my heart flutters and I smile back.

'I'm glad I came over today Kate. You've made me very happy.'

He puts his hand on mine and I breathe in deeply. He stands up to leave and I stand up to see him out. The shakes have left me and have been replaced by a euphoric buzz. He turns to face me and takes my face in both of his hands and we are standing an inch apart in my living room. My head is in a spin.

'So, let's work at being friends and build a relationship together?'

I nod but maintain eye contact. He leans forward. *What is he doing?* He kisses my forehead. *Ok, it's just the forehead.* Then he pulls my face and mouth to his and kisses me. I kiss him back, hard. His hands are holding my head like a prized possession and his mouth makes my knees weak. We don't kiss for long but it was long enough to leave a lasting impression.

'I don't want to go but I have to. I want you.'

I smile back at him like a love-struck teenager. We walk to the front door and we kiss briefly and he leaves. I close the door and then slide down it to the floor. *Holy fuck.*

Chapter 14

I spent the rest of that Sunday having the best hangover ever. Of course, I got straight onto the phone and told Ryan exactly what happened. He gave a mixed reaction.

'Well, I am glad you definitely aren't getting back with dickhead but I don't think going with your recently separated boss is your wisest move.'

'Don't piss all over my cornflakes Ryan. I'll be fine. It's just a bit of fun. We have both left something serious so no one is rushing into anything. It's fun and we all need a bit of fun in our lives don't we.'

'As long as that is all it is. Don't get carried away. Most people have a bit of fun yes but, this is you Kate. Everyone falls in love with you. Just be careful.'

'Well, I'm not one to brag' I joke with him on a complete high from my budding new romance. 'Are you coming over to watch a chick flick or not?'

'And listen to you harp on about Greg for the second night in a row? No thanks. I'm hanging anyway so it's an early night for me.'

'Ok. Night Ryan. Love you.'

'Love you too.'

I curled up on the sofa and waited for a pizza delivery. I chucked on Netflix and found a comedy come romance that was rated five stars that I decided to give a go, despite never agreeing with any of Netflix's ratings. About ten minutes in and already figuring out who was going to get with who I could see that this film wasn't going to capture my full attention. Just as well really as I was now in a full-on text conversation with Greg.

I felt warm and gooey and ridiculously happy. Was this a rebound? Would this end in tears? We get on so well, surely, we can both be adults about just having some fun? We would both be mad to rush into anything serious straight away. Plus, he needs to move out before we could ever have a proper relationship. As he's texting me I have found out they are all at home. They had some friends over for Sunday lunch and he is now watching a film with his youngest kid. Apparently, the wife is on the other sofa. It makes me feel weird knowing that they are all in the same room acting like a family. I suppose he just needs time. They have children to think about and I can't possibly relate. A couple of his texts have listed personal habits of hers that he doesn't like. I told him not to tell me that as I'm sure she could tell me a thing or two about him but from the tone of his messages it's clear that the marriage is dead in the water. How sad. They had twenty years together and two children. I suppose the only saving grace is that the children are older. I don't know if that's better or not. My parents separated before I can remember so I never knew any different but at least his two will have some memories they can cherish as a family. Maybe that makes it worse.

We are texting all evening. The credits have begun rolling on the film I was "watching" and I have no idea what happened. Presumably the guy got the girl. I have learned a lot about Greg this evening though. I have learned about how he is craving love and affection and says that he has been starved of it the last ten years. He says he wishes he was curled on the sofa with me. He says he hopes we have nights in together. He asks me if I would like that. We text about what TV and films we like and he ends up ordering a DVD on his amazon prime account and says it will be delivered tomorrow and that he is going to come over and we will watch it together. He certainly seems keen but I have always liked a man who knows what he wants and goes for it. Her loss is my gain, as they say.

The next morning, I awake early again. I cannot deny the excitement and nerves running through my system. I have to go into the office and act like I had a normal weekend when Greg and I will know that we were kissing in my living room less than twenty four hours ago. The buzz is addictive. I think about making a bit of extra effort whilst I get ready but then decide I would have to keep it up and I would prefer to look nice in my non-work gear so I go as I normally am, plus it seems to have worked so far.

This has to be the best Monday ever. The hangover is completely gone, I had a great night's sleep and now I am heading into the office where I hope to see my new love interest and swap naughty smiles. I can't help but sing along to every song on the radio and I don't care that the motorway is crawling again. I am on cloud nine and loving life. I can feel the cars around me laughing at me singing in my car, in fact there is a white van crawling along next to me which has a few men inside it and I am sure they are laughing at me but I don't care. No one is going to burst my bubble today and to be honest, how wonderful it is to feel this good on a Monday morning.

When I pull up into the car park I see his car there and I immediately start getting palpitations and my hands become clammy around the steering wheel. I can't wait to see him but at the same time I am so nervous I want to run away. There are only a couple of cars in the car park which means I will have to walk through a pretty empty office to my desk. Hopefully I can do that without tripping up or something. I begin to imagine getting my stiletto heel caught on a computer cable and clearing several desks as I belly slide across the floor causing third degree burns up my legs and then run out of the building in tears. *You can do this Kate, just walk slowly and carefully.*

As I enter the building and make my way in I can see him at his desk typing away. He senses someone approaching and looks up. When he realises it's me, he stops what he is doing and leans back in his chair and starts nibbling on his pen. Desire begins to run through my body and I try to not act coy but I can tell that I am blushing like a banshee.

'Good morning Mr Owen. How are we?'

'Miss Roberts. Very well and you?'

'Not bad, not bad at all.' I put my bags down on my desk and lean on the doorframe of his office. 'Can I get you a coffee?'

'That would be wonderful. You know how I like it, don't you?' He holds my stare.

'I think so but remind me.'

'Hot and on my desk.' I gulp and feel a rush of heat between my legs.

'Coming up.' I walk away as a colleague is approaching his office to speak to him. I know he is watching me walk away and once again I feel an immense pressure to walk sophisticatedly and pray that I can do so.

For the rest of that day I can't concentrate at work. I can feel him staring at me through the venetian blinds of his office and it makes me too nervous to even pick up the phone and call clients. I feel like I am on show. I'm consumed by shyness and feel extremely exposed. *This is ridiculous.* I can't stop thinking about what is going to happen next.

Just as I am pondering the many outcomes available one of the ladies is walking around with the post. Greg has his door shut and is in deep conversation with someone so Carol asks me to give Greg his mail when he has finished his meeting. She hands me a small pile and right on top is a package from Amazon. I know what it is. It's the DVD he ordered for us to watch tonight. I Pick it up and slowly run my fingers along the packaging, drifting off into a fantasy of him and I in coupled up bliss on the sofa. I catch myself behaving like a weirdo before my colleagues do, thankfully, and put the post down on my desk. As I look around I catch Greg's stare and he winks at me. He saw me with the DVD and he saw me daydreaming with it in my hand. He is loving this. He is loving this secret romance we are embarking on and I don't know how I feel about it. I'm normally an open, honest and chatty person and the one bit of news that I have and want to shout from the rooftops, I have to keep to myself. It's torture.

As the clock strikes five thirty I am out of there. Ok, as the clock strikes five twenty-nine I am out of there. I get home as fast as the traffic will allow and go through in my head what I need to do. Shower, spruce, make up, clothes. I need to look natural but hot. My heart is racing with the excitement. Sitting in that office all day knowing that we kissed the day before, knowing that my boss wants me and not being able to say a word was hard work. Although there is no one in the car with me I feel like I am free to scream with glee. One of the radio stations is playing eighties classics and they have never sounded better. I am beating along as if I have drumsticks, I am moving around whilst singing as if I have an audience, I am acting as if I'm... as if I'm in love.

Chapter 15

I pull up in my parking space and bolt out of the car, dropping my things as I try to move too hastily. I quickly pick them all up and shove them back into my bag. I can't remember the last time I rushed about for a man like this. I go into the block of flats and make my way quickly up the stairs but not too quickly as I want to be in one piece when he arrives and it is becoming apparent that I am quite hyper. I look at my phone and he has sent me a text me to say he will be leaving the office soon, by six at the latest. That gives me forty-five minutes depending on traffic. I expeditiously remove all my clothes and hop into the steaming shower. Hurriedly, I lather myself up in shower gel and scrub away my shame at having another man in my home so quickly after Tom leaving but that guilt lasts about two seconds. As I cleanse my body my hands get closer to my groin and I think what it would be like if he was in the shower with me. His confidence taking the lead and his hands running everywhere. With that thought in mind, I pull the shower head down. It doesn't take long. I am furiously aroused and feel like I could explode with excitement. I wonder what his touch will feel like on my body. I wonder if he will touch me tonight. I am consumed by curiosity of what this man is capable of, knowing that he already has my full attention with just one kiss.

Dried, dressed and looking naturally fresh I await my prince. He will be here any minute. I quickly grab a small glass of white wine and down it. I then wash up the evidence and rinse my mouth with mouthwash. I am shaking like a leaf. I want to see him but again, the nerves are so extreme I almost think about abandoning ship again. Too late. I see him pull up outside. I am having mild palpitations again and whilst giving myself the once over in the mirror I remind myself to get a grip and that nothing needs to happen. A few minutes pass and he still hasn't rung the buzzer. I go into the kitchen and try to peak out of the window without being seen that I am looking for him. He is talking to a woman that I see walking her dog around here.

'Huh, small world.' They wrap up their conversation and I see him look up at my flat window and then look back over his shoulder to where the woman is walking away. The buzzer rings and although I am stood right next to it, I casually let it ring a couple of times before allowing access to the building. To wait with the door open or not wait with the door open, that is the question. I don't have time to choose, he knocks the door to my flat. Now I am wishing I wasn't stood right behind it and so I feebly creep backwards, down the hallway, away from the door just so that I can heavily footed make my way back to the door, pretend I wasn't right behind the bloody thing waiting for him like the sad, pathetic, loser that I am.

'Hi!'

'Hey you.' He comes in straight away making me close the door behind him before kissing me briefly on the mouth. We separate and I offer a nervous giggle. *Goon.* He waves his Amazon package at me and gives me a smile.

'Movie night. Why don't you get the drinks and I will set it up.' He takes his coat off and makes himself extremely at home but I like it. He seems comfortable and I want him to feel that way. As I make my way into the kitchen to grab him a glass of wine, he is in the lounge closing the curtains and messing around with the TV. Anyone would think we had been together for years if they could see it. I feel a warm glow of contentment. It just seems to work. I feel at home with him in my home, surprisingly quickly. I still have to pinch myself that he is my boss and he is interested in me. It's straight out of Hollywood. He's mature, successful, has a flash car, seems to want to spend cosy nights in with me... he got here as quickly as he could and I like that. No games. He is a man who knows what he wants and seemingly, he knows how to get it.

I bring in two glasses of wine and get out some sophisticated nibbles. No tube of Pringles for this guy. I knew I had to be classier than that so at lunch time I went to a delicatessen in my teenage love-struck bubble. I picked up some mozzarella, sun dried tomatoes, chorizo and olives. He struck me as that kind of guy and I wanted to show him that despite the decent age-gap, I was a grown-up girl, if there was such a thing. As I lay out the spread on the coffee table he made no acknowledgment but pulled me into him, into the crook of his arm. I didn't mind his poor manners on this occasion, he was probably swept up in the moment just as I was. *I could make a point though...*

'Thanks for buying the DVD. You still haven't told me which one it is.'

'It's a crime drama that was on TV recently. It's fantastic. It's got that gorgeous mixed-race girl in it, that's what caught my attention but it ended up being really quite good.' I felt a pang of jealousy as he made his feelings clear for fancying another woman. Yes, we can all find another person attractive but do I want to hear about that right now? In the throes of a blossoming romance? Can't it wait until I am coming home from work to find you with your slippers on and one ball hanging out of your boxer shorts before you start throwing those comments around? *Get used to it Kate. They all window shop. As long as it's only looking.*

'Sounds great.' I offer a confident smile that says, *I am cool and calm, I don't mind you looking at other women.*

'Plus, they are only episodes, so if we miss bits, we can always go back.' He pulls my chin up to his mouth and kisses me again. 'I saw an old friend outside on my way in.'

'Oh, did you? Small world!'

'Yeah we went to school together. She walks the collie dog. Do you see much of her?'

'No but I know the one you mean. I see a lot of regular dog walkers but no one really talks to each other round here.'

He nods and picks up his wine and doesn't say anymore. For about forty minutes we sit in what becomes an awkward silence whilst watching his DVD. The tension is rip-roaringly loud and it is clear that this is still very new and no one wants to make the first move. I put my hand on his leg whilst standing up and picking up the wine glasses.

'Fancy another?'

'No, I can't I'm driving. I know what I do fancy though.' He pulls me down onto him and I place the glasses on the sofa, not caring whether a tiny dribble of white wine spills out. I am now straddling him and it seems we have quickly moved on. He takes my head in both his hands and pulls me in to kiss me hard. I kiss him back as hard as I can, making it clear that I want him. His hands begin to explore my body and I allow him. He teases me by gently stroking my torso and back with his fingers underneath my top. His soft fingers on my bare skin makes my body tingle. He pulls my top up and I raise my arms so he can remove it. He takes no time in unclasping my bra and cupping my breasts in his hands. Before I know it, his mouth is all over me and I stretch and moan in pleasure as his tongue explores my nipples with his hands firmly on my waist. I gyrate against his groin and feel him getting hard. Anything could happen right now and I hope it doesn't. I want to savour the moment. The first-time buzz and excitement can wear off all too quickly. I want us to stay in this frenzy of desire for as long as possible. I hope he doesn't try to take it further because I don't know if I will be able to refuse. I can't put my finger on it but I am not scared, I am not nervous. I have been transported to a world of wanderlust and we could be anywhere, anytime. I don't want to spoil this.

He kisses my breasts in his mouth as if he is kisses me, passionately sucking and licking. I arch my back and he leans in to me making sure not to let me go. I begin to massage my own head in the sheer eroticism of the moment, pulling my hair up on top of my head and moaning whilst rocking back and forth on him. This is enough. I do want more but I am getting enough out of this to wait. If he carried on a little longer I think I could actually climax just by what he is doing. We gradually reduce to halt and I collapse into him. I cradle him in my arms and we rock ever so slightly back and forth, his head nuzzling into my hair.

'You are some woman, Kate.'

'You are some guy... that mouth. Jeez.'

'Let's leave it there. I want to savour it.' *Oh my god, has he read my mind? We are in tune!*

I get dressed and see him off. He says he needs to get back and it is getting quite late. I am glad he is leaving. Although we have worked together for a couple of years, I am only just getting to know him and I will not and have not ever just jumped into bed with anyone. It's not my style. I need people to grow on me before I fancy them so one night stands have never been appealing. I think I could be on to something really quite magnificent here and I'm happy to take our time. As I have said before, we are both recently single. There is no need to rush. After he has left, I sink into the sofa and feel a warm glow all over my body. I want to pinch myself it seems so surreal. He seems like such a catch and I can't believe he is interested in me.

It sounds like his wife took him for granted based on what I know so far. I didn't see myself as a not far off thirty year old ending up with a forty something, divorced father of two but life has a funny way of working out. If this is what is meant for me, I'm taking it. So many marriages fall apart. Couples marry too young or the kids apply too much pressure or partners get neglected due to the job but whatever happened to them happened for a reason and now he is mine and although I can hardly quite believe it, I know I have never felt happier. He could be the one.

Tuesday comes and goes and I am glad we haven't planned to see each other. The intensity of my emotions and desire require a stop gap otherwise I will be putty in his hands. I cannot believe the hold he has over me already. I'm pretty sure it isn't a rebound. I've had rebounds, we all have but I can't remember ever feeling this way. I would say it's too good to be true but it's not.

There is a catch and that's what tells me it's worth it. We all know that if something is too good to be true then it is usually just that. The catch is he is still at home living with his family. The catch means the situation isn't perfect and the fact that it isn't perfect means it isn't too good to be true. That isn't his fault, it's just timing. He wanted to tell me how he felt whilst he knew I was single. I get that and I am happy to wait for him to sort his issues out. He has children and that has to be handled sensitively. I have just broken up from being a step parent so there is no need for me to have him here all the time and I can empathise with his situation.

Anyway, most of this is what I told Ryan on the phone last night. I love him to bits but he put a bit of a downer on things. He warned me that the marriage might not be over, that he could be lying to me. Or that he is using me to get back at his wife. I listened to what he had to say and although I could completely understand where he was coming from, I just wasn't getting that from Greg's behaviour. He seems so keen on me. He texts me frequently and even called me last night when he got home to say he was tucking himself into bed in the spare room and thanked me for a great night.

It's just complicated and life is complicated. Not everyone can just fall in to the perfect relationship, in the perfect circumstances and live, well, perfectly. It takes understanding and patience sometimes. He told me how cold and distant his wife had been for the last decade and I know he is terrified of how the kids will take it and what he needs is a good woman like me who will be waiting for him with open arms to help him through the storm. He can't possibly be lying to me, that would be stupid. He would have so much to lose. There is no way he is lying to me. *Is there?*

Chapter 16

My alarm went off and once again, I felt happy to be awake and indeed alive. Oh how wonderful it is to be in the throngs of a budding romance. As I pick up my phone to turn off the noise I see that I already have a text from Greg.

'Email the office and say you are working from home this morning. I'm coming over and I'm bringing breakfast. See you soon. G xxx'

'Shit!' I leap out of bed with more prowess than an Olympic Athlete attempting the pole vault and jump in the shower. Whilst in there I once again find myself aroused and would like to take my time but he could be here any minute so instead I speed things up slapping shower gel all over me and rinsing it off as if it's burning my skin. A quick scrub of my face trying to avoid getting any of the tiny little beads in my eyes and the once over with the razor under my arms. As I put the razor back on the shelf I take a quick glance downstairs and then feel my legs.

'No time and dangerous territory anyway, Kate!' Out of the shower and speedily back through to the bedroom, I apply my face when it occurs to me that I left the bathroom so rapidly that I could have paralysed myself. Jumping out of the shower like that, one false move and I could've broken my neck, pulling down the shower curtain with me as I fell and dislocated my leg for maximum bathroom trauma scene effect. As I ponder that thought I catch myself in the mirror frowning at the fear of my lucky escape and realise I don't look good frowning and tell myself that I must make an effort to not frown.

My mind wanders off again and I imagine lying on the bathroom floor in a heap with no one to help. Greg would arrive and he would be knocking on the door not realising I need his help but I can't call out because I'm unconscious. It would dawn on him that I hadn't replied to his text and he would think I was no longer interested and he would leave, believing he had been too assumptive and had blown it. Then, a snake that had been living in the loft and feeding off rats for the last six months would smell my broken body and sense my heat, would come slithering down through the pipework and somehow find its way out into the bathroom and would eat me. Eventually I would be found and there would be reporters surrounding the block of flats outside. The owner of the snake would be one of those residents that no one had seen before because he hibernates in his ground floor studio apartment with manky curtains that are always closed. He would be interviewed and he would say how happy he was to have his snake back as he thought he had lost him for good and then an image of my half-eaten by snake body with my modesty disguised by the shower curtain I pulled down during the tumble, would be shared around social media. I shudder at the thought and the doorbell rings. Cue accelerated heart rate, palms beginning to sweat and I wonder how long this buzz will last.

'Good morning Mr Owen, what a lovely surprise.'

'Miss Roberts.' As usual, he enters quickly and closes the door promptly whilst kissing me on the cheek which I feel with a pang of disappointment as it is not on the mouth. 'Quick question, well favour? Can I use your car parking space out the back?'

'Yeah, I will need to go and move it. Why?'

'Well, having seen Rachel, the woman from school yesterday it just reminded me it's a small world. I don't want Kirsty finding out about us yet you know, it's delicate.'

I look at him and don't say anything. He takes my chin in his hand and pulls me close, 'Don't worry. It's just that the kids don't know yet and plus, although it was a mutual decision, I don't want to rub her face in it. When she sees you, she will be extremely jealous of you so we just need to tread carefully for a while, ok?'

'Yeah ok. That makes sense. I don't want to bulldoze my way in. I'll go and move my car now and you can use my space.'

He kisses me on the forehead. 'There's a good girl.' My toes curl. I cannot bear being called a good girl. I will have to train him out of that.

Once back inside, as if a switch has been flicked he kisses me furiously. His hands are everywhere and he is making no mystery of his desires for me. We kiss and kiss and kiss. His hands on my hips, up and down my back, in my hair, on my face. He pulls me into him and I know he wants me to feel how hard he is. I want to take it further but something is holding me back.

I think this is the real deal but for some reason I have a fear within me and so I don't explore him. I just kiss him. I kiss him passionately then tenderly and back to passionately. We kiss for so long it's as if we are teenagers. Teenagers desperate to go to the next base but terrified because we don't know what we are doing.

Gradually I release my lips from his and lead him to the kitchen, taking baby steps and giving him baby kisses. I don't want a dramatic stop, I want him to know I am interested but we need to be careful. We have to consider we work together and that he is my boss. I have to consider I have just called off my engagement. He has to consider he has just ended his sixteen-year marriage. His love is so addictive that I don't want to have to deal with a horrific comedown. We have to take our time. I make us some filter coffee and we begin to talk. I begin to feel normal as the situation becomes more normal and civilised. Yes, I wanted to get undressed with him but first thing in the morning before my colleagues are even logging on at their desks just seemed odd.

He tells me about the meetings he has that day and we talk about maybe getting away for a weekend. Away from work, away from his broken marriage. A place where we can be us... without upsetting anyone. I feel excited and knowing that he wants us to go away together so soon makes me feel confident that he is serious. This isn't him just wanting his leg over, he is talking to me about a day out in London, taking in the sights, being anonymous and then eventually, we both know it, being hurled up in a hotel room together undisturbed. I agree that it sounds like a wonderful idea and he says he will have a look on-line at some options.

After our coffee, he says he must make a move to get to his meeting on time but not before some more heavy petting. I can't remember kissing like it before. It is non-stop and it doesn't become boring. I want to keep kissing him and it reminds me that kissing dies out of a relationship. It's a new relationship thing. Heavy kissing until you've gone all the way a few times and the kissing becomes less and the sex becomes more.

I've always been complimented on my kissing. I don't see it as a means to an end. I think you can tell quite a lot about a partner by the way they kiss. I start off with gentle kisses only allowing the mouth to open a little. Soon after I let the tongue slip in but not much. Then I kiss harder and maybe gently bite the bottom lip. Then, open the mouth more and insert more tongue. I like the tongues to brush each other gently. I don't want a messy tongue everywhere, I want it soft, slow, teasing. I want him to show me how he uses it as it will have its uses elsewhere later. I like to hold the back of their head and hold them close to me and press my body against theirs whilst all the time opening my mouth more, giving more tongue and pressing hard. That's how I like to kiss.

We end up on my bed. I know it's safe as he has to leave for his meeting in five minutes. He is on top of me and he is pushing his groin against mine. Just as I have shown him how I like to kiss, he is showing me how he likes to make love. He begins to kiss my neck. My weak spot. I moan as he pushes his tongue into the crook of my neck, nuzzling deep, gently groping a breast all whilst dry humping me. The build-up is immense. If he began to undress me now I know I would surrender. I gyrate back, groin to groin, rocking together. I wrap my legs around his waist, my hands in his hair, his mouth on my skin. We are both acting as if it is happening but we are fully clothed.

Eventually, just when I am beginning to wonder if I could reach climax doing this he pulls away.

'Christ, that was something.' He rolls over on to his back as if he has just finished.

'Yeah, that was quite something.'

'I want you, Kate Roberts.' I roll over, straddle him and look him in the eyes;

'You can have me, Greg Owen.'

We kiss again but more delicately so.

'Don't go in to the office. Stay here. I will come back after my meeting.'

He peeled his body off mine and we kiss all the way to the door where I see him out and we sheepishly grin at each other. My body is tingling with excitement and anticipation. We both know what will happen when he comes back and this could seal the deal. So far, he is ticking a lot of boxes but will he be able to satisfy me and me him? Will he be of a good size? Will we be a good fit? Will we click. If our dry humping is anything to go by then the chemistry is definitely there. I just pray that he doesn't have a pencil penis, a shitake mushroom where his cock should be or on the other end of the scale, some kind of Trojan penis that makes me want to run for the hills.

I couldn't be sure how long he would be. He could be back in an hour or two hours. In two hours, we could be back on that bed, rocking together but without any clothes on and whilst I ponder that thought goose bumps appear everywhere. I have this short window to do some work emails and be seen to be working and find something casual but sexy to put on. I want to make it look like I am dressing down but in a way that makes him want to ravish me. I have just the number. A little strappy, black t-shirt dress.

He knocked the door and I found myself practising some breathing techniques before I answered. He wants me and I want him. The ardent build up was very real and again, I felt like I could back out instead of going through with this because the nerves were so substantial. After what seemed like a reasonable amount of time to keep him waiting I

prise open the door and there are no words. He pounces on me. Closing the door quickly, his mouth is on mine and his hands are everywhere.
'You are fucking gorgeous.'
'So are you.'
The kissing is loud and wet and we feed each other compliments in between whilst he forces me to walk backwards to the bedroom. Now we are on the bed and the breathing is becoming heavier. He is on top of me and we are grinding again. Kissing, exploring and stroking each other everywhere. I sit up and take control. I straddle him and pull him up so I am nose to nose with him. I begin to undo his shirt and kiss his neck. He tilts his head back and groans. I now have his shirt completely undone and peel it off him. He has a six pack. I wasn't expecting that. A six pack and a nice amount of body hair. Not quite silverback, not quite teenager. I've always liked a bit of hair and then I remember how Tom had none on his torso or his head for that matter. *Don't think about Tom, now is not the time.*

Greg pushes me down and pulls my legs out from beneath me and I'm on my back again. He wastes no time in completely undressing me. I'm naked and he is in his boxers. His mouth is on my breasts and I can see he is enjoying what he's doing as much as I am. He is French kissing my breasts and the euphoria is overwhelming. He makes his way down to my navel and looks me in the eye. He slowly sucks his index finger whilst maintaining eye contact and then inserts it in me. I throw my head back and arch my shoulders and open my legs wider for him. I come quickly and want more. He looks at me and grins before lowering his mouth down to me. Beginning slowly, he gently strokes me with his tongue around the outside and then up and down and then in. He keeps looking at me to see if he's doing it right and I raise my hips to him to make him continue. My hands are in his hair and my hips rock in time with his tongue. He's gentle and I like that. These things shouldn't be rushed. He's taking his time. He's taking care of me first. I know how this works. The excitement for him means the first time will be quick so he wants to put in a good show for me first and it's working. I play with my nipples as he gets me wetter and I decide I can't wait any longer. I close my legs and pull him up towards me. He is already taking off his boxer shorts and he reveals a beautiful looking penis. The relief is momentous. He looks thick and a good length and he looks bloody hard.

He hovers above me and we kiss tenderly. It's a different kiss to all the others we have had. He's being a gentleman and letting me know that he is soft and caring. He is about to say something when I take him in my hand and guide him in. We both moan and he slowly begins. He is so thick, much bigger than Tom and I feel well and truly spoilt. He now ticks all the boxes. I rock my hips in time with him. He kisses my neck and I gently scratch his back. With each moan, I can tell he is fighting to hold back. I pull his mouth to mine and we kiss and begin to move faster. Faster and faster, harder and harder. I observe his whole body. His muscly arms, his big manly legs, his ripped torso and I can't believe he wants me. My whole body is writhing in pleasure and I am there. I moan loudly and tell him softly in his ear that I have come and he joins me instantly. He thrusts hard, head back, arms taught and says, 'Oh baby. Oh baby. Oh baby!' before collapsing on top of me. As he does he pulls me in tight and continues to slowly rock until we reach a stop and just lie there, holding each other.

Chapter 17

The next two weeks pass in a blissful haze with a plethora of risqué picture messages, a pinch of descriptive messages and more sex than you can shake a stick at. Greg finds the time to see me every day. He either asks me to work from home and visits me during the day or he comes round for the evening but that is less frequent. I had mentioned to him that I would love it if we could wake up together and he says he has a surprise for me tonight.

He never talks about what is happening at home with Kirsty. All I know is that he always needs to be home by 10:30pm. He tells me things are strained and tense and I feel bad for him. He regularly tells me what a terrible wife she is and how she has taken him for granted for years and now the light is at the end of the tunnel, he cannot bear what it will do to their children. I make sure he feels good when he comes to mine. I want him to see that things will get better and that all the commotion will calm down and that I can offer him a safe place, a warm embrace when he wants it.

He tells me how different I am from her and I wish he wouldn't. I think Tom is a prick but none of his friends would believe what I could tell them. I think all relationships are capable of bringing out bad traits in people and so I don't think it's fair for an ex-partner to evaluate an individual's being. Of course, it would be a negative review and an extremely personal one that no one else could relate to. The relationship didn't work so that leaves a negative result and in my experience most men can't take the blame so it always ends up being the woman who was the psycho. I don't respect people who claim to have only dated psycho's previously. As if they are Mr Perfect. It's more refreshing to hear 'She was great, we just grew apart' or 'We just weren't compatible.' Why does it always have to be, 'I had a lucky escape / she was a psycho / all my friends and family hate her'. When Tom described his ex-wife as that to me, I should've known he was the problem and ran a mile so now I am extremely wary.

Greg doesn't talk about Kirsty that badly, he just tells me how they haven't had sex for almost a decade, live in separate bedrooms, how boring she is, she drinks too much gin, spends all his money and is at times, lazy with the kids. I feel that I don't have the right to know these intimate insights to her persona and unless I can see that he needs to talk it out, I ask him not to tell me the details. It's none of my business and I'm not stupid. I'm sure she could tell me a thing or two about him. The crux of it is, is that they just aren't happy together anymore. At least they can see that and have ended it and once he has healed properly, we can move forward publicly and appreciate each other. I hope she finds the same. It sounds to me like she was incredibly unhappy as well so them separating is for the best plus, kids aren't stupid. They will have sensed this outcome for some time. They have probably spoken to their school friends about it and know it's only a matter of time.

Everyone deserves to be happy. Of course, she is not going to be happy that Greg has moved on so quickly with me when she hasn't met anyone yet and perhaps he should've waited to move out of their home but no one is perfect. Life isn't perfect.

Tonight, Greg arrives a little later at around 8:30pm. We end up in bed together almost instantly. It has become clear that Greg is old fashioned in bed. He likes to be in control, doesn't want anything too wild and I get the distinct impression he is making up for a lack of sex in his life. I am happy to oblige and luckily for him, he has enough girth that he doesn't need to make much of an effort anyway. I'm still not completely comfortable with the 'Oh baby' routine every time he comes but he's man who knows what he wants, what he likes and I find that sexy. Afterwards he jumps in the shower and I go to get him a beer and prepare some snacks.

'Oh no thanks babe, I don't have time tonight. I need to get back to the boys. Kirsty and I have things to discuss so I said I wouldn't be late.'

My face drops and he can see what I am thinking.

'I'm sorry, I don't mean to rush off but I couldn't not see you. You have been on my mind all day.' He cups my face with his hands and kisses my forehead. 'I also wanted to see you so that I could tell you what I have organised. Next week I am taking you away to a luxury hotel. Five star. Just you and me all night *and* we can wake up together.'

He looks at me and I offer him a smile despite the knot in my stomach.

'Sounds amazing. Can't wait.'

'It'll be great. I will tell you more tomorrow.' And just like that he has gone. I don't feel good. Far from it. I feel used. He came in, had sex with me and darted. I want to speak to someone but I can't. The only person I would tell is Ryan but I am afraid he will tell me something I would rather not hear. Instead, I pour myself a glass of wine and curl up on the sofa trying not to let my imagination run wild. As if he read my mind, a text comes in.

'I'm sorry gorgeous. I would've loved to stay but I also need to make changes at home so we can be together. This meeting is about that. I hope you understand. I want you. Grrrr. G xxx'

I feel slightly better. I know he has a lot on his plate. I just would've preferred it if we hadn't had sex on this occasion. Not if there isn't time to talk afterwards. This isn't a fuck and duck service.

I am disappointed the next morning to not wake up to a text from him. Every morning since this three-month fling began, he has texted me first thing. I make a point of not texting him first and the sting from his fuck and duck behaviour last night resurfaces. *Ouch.*

I make my way into the shower and begin the mornings ablutions. I suppose I am female, I over analyse everything. I should give the guy a break. Let's look at it realistically. Why would he not text me this morning when he usually does? He got up late and has had to rush out to a meeting? *I would still find time to send a text. Shut up Kate, give the man a chance.* One of the kids is poorly and he is tied up with that? *Doesn't stop him from sending a text.* He had a huge row with Kirsty last night and is in a mood? *Most likely reason so far.* He ended up in bed with Kirsty… *Oh shut up! Uuuurgh!* I shake my head to try and rid it of the thought. I tell myself I am being stupid. He is not with Kirsty. If he was, he was playing a dangerous game and he would be risking his whole family set up by being with me. He doesn't strike me as that kind of guy. He wouldn't deliberately hurt and use people, he's a nice guy. They probably had a row.

By the time I have finished getting ready, had breakfast and was getting into my car I was still mulling over the possibilities. Sometimes I hate being a woman. Why do we get so attached? Why can't we just fuck like a man? Why does it always have to be about love?

When I pull up in the car park, Greg's car is there. He wasn't late for a meeting then. He obviously wanted to get out of the house though. They must have had a row. *Stop. Torturing. Yourself. Kate.*

'Morning Kate! How are we today?' He seems bright and breezy.

'I'm good thanks, you?' I ask inquisitively.

'I'm great.' *Why is he great?* I sit down and fire up my station and prepare for the day. Whilst I wait for my archaic computer to load up I begin chewing on my pen as I look at my pipeline that I have printed off and pinned to my cubicle.

'Looking good.' He is standing right behind me.

'What?' My heart is fluttering.

'Your pipeline. Looks good. You're easily the best sales person I've seen this morning.'

'I'm the only one in.' I say unimpressed by his crap joke. As I turn round, he hands me his empty coffee cup.

'Thanks, you're my favourite salesperson.' Then just like that he walks off. Does he think I am his office bitch? He is beginning to piss me off but like a good little girl, off I go and make his lordship his coffee. Black. One and half spoons. No sugar. He won't be getting any sugar from me either today. *Prick. Why do all men let their standards slip once they have you? Why can't they see that we don't become a psycho if they stay as the man they were when we met. Uuurgh. This is the Mondayest Wednesday ever.*

Graham the caretaker comes in to the kitchenette whilst I am making the drinks.

'Morning Graham! Fancy a coffee?'

'Morning Princess. That would be lovely. You seem bright and cheerful as always. You light up this office, you know that Kate.'

'It's all a façade, trust me!'

Greg appears.

'Break it up you two, people will start talking.' He winks at me as if he is clever. What is it with him this morning. His humour is on par with a five-year old. I pass him his coffee.

'Here you are your highness.'

'Your highness? I like it. Good to know you all know your place.' He winks again and walks off, then turns and comes back. "Careful though, the sparks between you two could start a kitchen fire.'

Graham looks at him with disgust as he walks off. 'He is such a prick. What is his problem?'

'I think that is his attempt at being funny. Don't worry, I didn't think it was funny either but we've all got to humour the boss man... unfortunately.' I chink his cup with mine as if they were beers. 'How are things at home? How is Linda?'

'She's not great. I thought once she had gotten the all clear that things would improve but she seems so depressed. Her hair is back all over now but she says she looks like Sinead O'Connor and that's still getting her down.'

I squeeze his arm. 'It will just take a bit of time. She will come back to you. You have both been through the mill. Hang in there.'

'Thanks Kate. You're one of the only genuine people in this office.'

'Well, I'm not one to brag.' I smile cheekily.

'And the most modest!'

'Ah that's why you love me.'

'Don't encourage me. I haven't had sex for fourteen months.'

'Ooooooooh kaaaay. Time to get on with work.' We walk off in separate directions both chuckling but mine is insincere. *Do all men fall out of love if they aren't getting sex? His wife had cancer for fucks sake. Men! Love your woman!*

I sit down at my desk to find that my piece of shit computer needs to update. That will take most of the morning. This company invests no money in its staff or equipment yet they want me to go out and sell our services. It's ridiculous. I might as well turn up to my meetings with a slab of slate and chalk and sell what we do through a series of hieroglyphics and the medium of dance.

Whilst I wait for it, it's on 2%, I begin to analyse again. Why did Greg come to the kitchen? He knew I was making him a coffee and would take it to him? Was he trying to break up the conversation between Graham and I? Graham was no threat. He was a bit of an office pest but he wasn't much of a catch. The rest of the team gradually appeared, each of them bringing in their own noise and commotion. Moaning about traffic, poor sleep and just an overall lacklustre level of energy for the day ahead.

In Britain, the only day that the office works to capacity is on a Thursday. Monday to Wednesday is spent looking for other jobs, get rich quick plans and generally moaning about life and the weather. Thursday is a hive of activity as the weekend becomes more believable and Friday is frittered away with plans for their forty-eight hour sabbatical.

I get the lethargy consensus for work. None of us get paid enough to have the life we want but the constant weather updates get on my nerves. This is Britain! Even in summer you need a rain coat, a jumper and your shorts. It's been this way for an incredibly long time. Why are you all having such trouble adjusting! It's safer to assume it won't be hot. Just have an emergency summer outfit in the boot of your car. Problem solved.

After a typical Wednesday at work I pack up my things and look at my phone. Nothing from Greg. No text telling me to rush back and wait for him in bed. No text from Greg asking if I have dinner plans.

Nothing. *Maybe he did sleep with Kirsty last night?* I don't like how I feel and I tell myself I am being irrational but I can't help but feel that something is up. He has been in a great mood all day but he sped off last night and hasn't text me once today which isn't like him at all. Pissed off and fed up, I leave the office without saying goodbye to anyone. I refuse to sit in and feel sorry for myself so I send a text out to the troops.

'Pub tonight anyone?'

'Yes! Xx'

'Defo! Xx'

'Best idea I've heard all day xx' Good. Most of the gang are up for it. I rev up my engine and see Greg leaving the building. I pretend I haven't seen him and speed off. I accidentally speed off too hard and do a wheel spin. Cringe.

I race home and chuck a microwave meal for one on whilst I jump in the shower. Once out I pull on some ripped jeans and a loose blouse. Best bit of advice I got from one of my gay friends was that men don't like women who look like they take hours to get ready. They prefer the low key but sexy look. Works for me because I can't be arsed with hair and wear minimal make up. I don't have problems attracting men admittedly. Just the right ones.

Taking my mechanically reclaimed lasagne out of the microwave whilst trying not to burn myself I am startled by a knock at the door. I drop the disgusting looking meal on the side whilst sucking on my finger that feels burnt. I am not expecting any visitors and you have to ring the intercom so it must be a neighbour after some sugar or something. I look through the peephole to see a bunch of flowers taking up the view. Gingerly, I open the door.

'Hey gorgeous girl.' It's Greg and he's brought wine too. 'They are not roses I'm afraid. They are the best that Waitrose had.'

'They are lovely, thank you.' I take them from him and kiss him on the lips. He puts his hands on my hips and makes his way into the flat. I feel like I am beginning to notice that he is quite domineering. Not overbearing but I might need to keep an eye on this. He is clearly used to having his own way.

'Your arse looks great in those jeans.'

'Why thank you. I don't have long I'm afraid, I'm on my way out.'

'Oh.' He looks crestfallen.

'Sorry, meeting the gang at the pub.'

'I didn't realise. I thought you stayed in during the week and it's raining. What about your hair?'

'I don't *always* stay in and who cares about my hair, the pub has a roof.'

'When are you going?'

I look at my watch. 'About five minutes ago.'

He picks up my meal for one and judges it and me. 'What is this shit?'

'It's called marinated living alone drizzled with don't have time to cook.'

'It looks like cat sick. I thought we could get a take away. I brought wine.' He gives me puppy dog eyes.

'Thanks. I can see that but I wasn't expecting to see you. It helps if you notify people of your intentions I find. I might be many things but a mind reader isn't one of them.'

'Yeah ok. Well stay here for a bit. Go later.'

'No. I said I would be there at seven.'

'It's 6:15pm.' He pulls me in with a boyish cheeky grin. 'We've got forty-five minutes.' He kisses me and starts nibbling my neck. I prise myself out of his grip.

'No, we don't. I need to be there in forty-five minutes.'

'That's loads of time.' He pulls me back and begins more nibbling and now his hands are everywhere.

'I can't. I felt like crap last night when you left. I don't want you coming here just to have sex with me. That doesn't make me feel good. If we don't have time to lie together afterwards or have the whole evening together then I'm not doing it.'

He looks like he's had his toys taken away from him.

'Ok, I understand.'

'Don't be like that. I haven't heard from you since last night. You normally text and you haven't today and then you turn up unannounced hoping for more sex? That is not how things are going to work.' He looks pissed off now.

'I am not using you for sex. I am not a monster, I just thought you would be free and be pleased to see me. I do have the whole evening free, I wanted to spend it with you.'

'I would've have loved to… had I known but I have plans now.'

'Alright, alright. Can I give you a lift to the pub then?' I smile and nod and before I know it we are kissing passionately and he is taking my clothes off and I'm not stopping him. *God, I'm weak.*

Weak I was, moody I was no longer. I know I should've stood my ground but it's not like I didn't gain anything either. He didn't use me if that's what you're thinking. I got four amazing orgasms and I do enjoy watching him having his pleasure. Anyway, he knows how I feel now. If he tries it again then I will know he hasn't listened to me. I need to give the guy a chance. I jump out of bed and he slaps my backside whilst biting his bottom lip.

'You turn me on so much!' He says almost shouting and slapping the steering wheel. We are in what I like to call his passion wagon and I feel smug that this man wants me and he is taking me to see my friends. This grown man with his super sexy sports car and his confidence. He knows what he wants, there is no denying that. He pulls up round the back of the pub and takes my head in both hands and kisses me hard.

'Be good. Have fun and I'll see you in the morning.'

'Thanks, thanks and thanks for the lift.'

We kiss and I vacate the sexy sports car. It purrs like a tiger. I've never been into cars but I even find his car has sex appeal. How does that work?

'Kate?'

'Yeah?' I lean down to see him in his bucket style seat.

'You are smoking hot.'

Kalopsia

I smile, blow him a kiss and close the door. *So are you Greg Owen. So are you.*

Chapter 18

'What the fuck? What the actual fuck?' I am pacing the hallway and he looks like he has been kicked in the balls.

'It was booked before we started this. It's nothing to worry about. It's just a trip for the boys, my children.'

'Nothing to worry about? You are going to America for a two and a half-week holiday with your wife and it's nothing to fucking worry about? Fuck you Greg!'

'I promise you Kate, please calm down. I don't want to be with her. I don't want to go! It's just that…'

'It's just that what? That you can't fucking say no? This is asking too much. Way too much. I have tried my best to accept your situation but I do not accept this. Two and a half fucking weeks? Who goes on a family holiday for two and a half fucking weeks? I thought you hated each other?'

'We do. Well we don't but we do if you know what I mean.'

'No. I don't know what you mean Greg. I couldn't possibly understand what you mean. I want you to leave.'

'Kate. Please. No. Don't do this. We can figure it out.'

'Get out. Get. The. Fuck. Out.' I manhandle him out of the door without looking at him and close it firmly behind him and lock it. I walk through to the kitchen and I can hear the blood circulating in my ears, the pressure sounds like the ocean swooshing in my head. I place my hands apart widely on the worktop and lower my head. My heart is racing. I feel numb one minute and like I could explode the next. I feel like I could scream. I feel like I could cry. I will do neither.

After a few deep breaths, I get my bag and hunt for my mobile phone. I dig and search frantically. Handbags; great for storing crap but bad because all the crap hides whatever it is you are looking for. I lose my temper and empty the contents of the bag on the kitchen floor. The usual suspects can be seen. An old packet of tissues that have never been resealed properly so are probably more likely to cause an infection that clean up a runny nose. A hairband. Half a polo mint. Loose change that is from this country and a euro. An old train ticket. My diary. A lip balm that I forgot I had. I remove the lid to look at it and as suspected it had come loose from its lid at one point and is now covered in fluff and tobacco. Tobacco crumbs from moments of weakness. A cigarette would be good right now. A hairbrush. My purse that is currently as empty as my heart. A reusable shopping bag. Business cards and a leaflet offering me a free shot at a nightclub that I couldn't say no to from a young girl in the street.

I admire anyone who is trying regardless of if I want their services or not. The club in question is a 'wipe your feet on the way out' kind of venue so I would never drink there but I thanked her for the offer anyway. My phone.

I immediately call Ryan knowing that the only way I can survive the day is to fill it with distraction. I am not strong enough to mull over what that man is up to right now. He is under my skin and it's dangerous.

'Hey bitch, what the fuck do you want?'

'Good. I'm glad you are around. I need to busy myself today. Are you free for afternoon cocktails in town? I'm not going to lie, it could get messy.'

'Sounds like my perfect Saturday afternoon. I said I would meet a couple of others today, you haven't met them. Can they come? Nice gays, you will love them.'

'Yeah sure. The more, the merrier. Literally.'

'Great. When and where?'

'I'll get the bus in forty-five minutes and will be at Coco Loco in an hour. First one there gets the first round. Make mine an espresso martini to begin.'

'Same. Same.

'Love you, bye.'

'Love you, bye.'

It doesn't take long to get ready. I was already dressed up for Greg coming over for brunch. I had been to the hairdressers and got them to do a blow-out first thing before he came over, made passionate and sensual love to me and then told me he was going to America in two weeks... for two and a half weeks. After a quick shower, I slipped on a loose summer dress. One of those ones that I always classed as casual but always seemed to get compliments when I wear it. I could fuss for hours over choosing a 'hot' outfit and not get one compliment but get ready in a rush and seem to get it right. It's not on purpose, I'm just one of those girls. I'm not very good at really dressing up. I'm crap at applying make-up so hardly ever bother and I'm not comfortable in really girly clothing. Skinny jeans and a blouse suits me any day.

I know that my phone has been going off with numerous messages but for the first time in a couple of months I don't bother looking. I know it's him and I don't want to hear what he has to say until I have heard what Ryan has to say. I think I already know what Greg has to say for himself and unfortunately, I think I know what Ryan will have to say too.

On the bus on the way into town I plug in some music in my continued efforts to not listen to my own thoughts. The first song that comes on is Bryan Adams – Run to you and after a minute or so of listening to the words intently, I want to launch my phone down the aisle of the bus.

She says her love for me could never die. But that'd change if she ever found out about you and I. Oh but her love is cold, wouldn't hurt her if she didn't know, 'cause when it's all too much, I need to feel you touch. I'm gonna run to you.

I take in every word and wonder if this is what I am caught up in. Has he been lying to me? He has told me she doesn't know about me but that they have separated. Could be bullshit. He is staying for the kids for the time being. Could be bullshit. He is having his cake and eating it. Probably most likely. I remove my earphones and turn the music off. I am going to find messages in every song I hear so I decide to zone out to the cacophony of bus chatter.

Coco Loco is buzzing with everyone out making the most of one of the few summer days we seem to get. I'm lucky to get a table which means I can't go up and order a drink through fear of losing it and if there's one thing you can say about the brits it's don't count on them leaving a bar anytime soon on a summers day. The people that are already enjoying an early cocktail will be the same people here at 10pm tonight talking much louder than they are now and stumbling all over the place and being so loud that at times you won't be able to tell if there is trouble or if they are happy. That's what fourteen or more Caribbean cocktails can do to a person.

Whilst patiently sitting and strolling through a tedious news feed of nothing important but equally addictive gossip on Facebook I hear the sound of a skate boarder getting very close to me and look up to see the tall, dark and handsome heartbreaker of an ex of mine, Jake. The ex before Tom. The ex that I couldn't see a future with. The ex that I didn't believe loved me. The ex that I didn't think was grown up enough. The ex that was the best lover I've ever had. Honestly, this man blew sex out of the water compared to most men. By the time Tom and I were over, there was no foreplay and I was lucky if I got five minutes out of him. Even luckier if he stayed hard for the full five minutes but more often than not, it was two minutes and it was always in the dark. He couldn't bear to have the lights on because he told me I put him off. What a wanker. It's one thing to be insecure but don't try and bring everyone else down with you.

'Hey Kate, how are you?' He skidded to a smooth and stylish stop next to me and picked up his board. I stood to greet him. We cuddled and pecked each other's cheeks. He felt good. I had forgotten what it was like to be with a tall man. I could have nuzzled right into the nook of his protruding collar bone very easily and allowed myself to pretend for a dreamy moment that we were still together but he pulled away quickly. He was always respectful.

'I'm really good. It's lovely to see you, want to join me for a drink whilst I wait for my friends?'

'Yeah sure, why not.'

I watched his every move as he put his skate board down and glided onto the bench opposite me. His distinctly chiselled features seemed more prominent than usual, I found myself wanting to touch his jawline which was one of the many things that attracted me to him. He has a strong jawline, wolf like blue eyes and jet black, dark, curly hair. He was my Mr Darcy. My modern day, skateboarding, nonchalant Mr Darcy. I had been staring at him making his own rolled cigarette when he suddenly felt my eyes on him and stopped what he was doing.

'Sorry, how rude of me. Do you want me to make you one?'

'Yeah that would be great. Actually, I'll go and grab us a drink. What do you want, beer?'

'Yeah. That would be awesome. Thanks, Kate.'

I came back laden with drinks and casually gave him his as I sat down. I wondered if he could detect that I was reminising his body, his touch, his ways. Who was I kidding. He wouldn't have a clue what I was thinking. That was one of the reasons we broke up, because he never knew what I was thinking and was always miles away from how I was feeling. We passed the time by catching up over trivial news and at times the conversation became stifled. Not out of not caring, perhaps he was wondering what I was thinking just like I was wondering what he was thinking. Was he imagining kissing me once more? Was he hoping that we could end up between the sheets for old times sakes? We were pretty good at that. Was he picturing us together in a naked embrace as I was?

As the conversation became stagnant, Ryan arrived with his friends and changed the dynamics entirely. Jake was an introvert and spoke almost in a whisper. He would draw you in forcing you to give him your full attention. Ryan was loud and animated and gregarious. Jake couldn't cope with Ryan's levels of enthusiasm. Ryan clocked him and gave me a look sharply followed by a roll of the eyes before announcing he was going to get some drinks. Jake made his excuses and left and kissed me on the cheek.

'Give me a shout if you're still out later.' He skated off before I could reply. I wanted to tell him I could be out later if he wanted me to be.

Ryan came back and did a quick look around the area, 'Thank fuck he's gone. What are you talking to that prick for?'

'Oh, he's alright. We were just saying hi. Nothing else. Promise.'

'Good. He's a loser. Who goes around on a skateboard anyway.'

'Better that than with his on/off wife.'

'Right. Spill. What the fuck is happening?'

With many interruptions, I finally bring Ryan up to speed with Greg's holiday plans. To say he is not happy is an understatement. He demands that I end it immediately. He suggests visiting his wife and 'outing' him. He proposes we follow him. All of his offers are fairly normal in the circumstances I suppose but I tell him that I won't entertain any of them. Of course, I am worried, of course I am concerned but I believe in trusting someone until you have a good reason not to. He knows I am not happy and I want to see what will happen next. I don't' want to end it in case he is being faithful to me. Maybe it is just one last holiday. They have kids to think about. I don't. He has made promises to me and as yet, he has not broken them so perhaps for now I just have to suck it up and deal with it. It's complicated and I always knew it would be so I decide to give him the benefit of the doubt. I haven't told him that yet. First, I am going to have more cocktails than I need and then I will speak to him after making him sweat. I might also see what Jake is up to later.

The afternoon flowed into the early evening and the guy's company was just what I needed. I was now suitably numb and had enjoyed their stories to distract me from my troubled mind. Saying that, I couldn't repeat much of what was said because I wasn't really listening but it was the perfect distraction. The perfect antidote for concerns of infidelity. I was on the brink of too much alcohol and beginning to feel sorry for myself. Only I could remove myself from one toxic relationship straight into one with an unavailable man. I replayed the laughs we had shared so far and the intimate moments and told myself it couldn't just be sex. He had talked to me. He had talked to me more in three almost four months than Tom had done in two and a half years. I knew there was something to this. I just had to give him time. Then my mind took me to a picture of him and her together and it was like being woken up on the operating table as the scalpel is about to plunge in.

'I'm going. I need to get ready for my date.' Ryan was grinning, clearly excited about the evening ahead as to whether this could be his last ever first date.

'Oh, please don't go. Sack it off. He will be a prick, just like the rest of them.'

'I'm going. This one is hot. I am definitely going.'

'Hot. That will be temporary. Give it a few months. Once he's under your skin he will start messing you about. Start controlling you, telling you what you can wear and probably have a wife.'

'Nah. I don't pick pricks like you Kate. My Prickdar is in full working order. I'm going. You need to as well. You look sad.'

'I am not going. I am not going to go home and sit on my own wondering if my new boyfriend is still having it off with his wife. Just when I thought this year couldn't get any more fucked up.'

'Has he text you?'

'Holy shit. He has. Twelve times!' My heart starts beating again out of nowhere and I ponder for a minute if it had almost flat lined.

'Well that means one of two things. He realises he has fucked up and is desperate to make it right or, he knows you are on to him and wants to fuck with you a little bit more. Be careful. Stay out then, find someone to hang out with but text me and stay safe.' He kisses me on both cheeks and like the little hurricane that he is, he leaves as quickly as he came.

There is no way I am going home. It's 6pm. Admittedly I am six cocktails in and haven't eaten yet but I know if I go home I might as well buy some cats on the way and be done with it. I choose an even sadder option and decide to stay out on my own. Can women do that? Do I care right now? I leave the seat and head up to my old local from when I lived in town. There are two reasons for this. One, it is on the way to my bus stop and two, it is Jake's local.

I realise as I make the short walk there that I am fairly tipsy. There is a wide selection of sub-standard eateries on the way to choose a light snack from. A kebab shop, a burger joint, a cheap pizza parlour, the obligatory 'chicken land' that can be found in any city near the favourite watering holes. I opt for a Tesco express and buy a wrap. I might be tipsy but I am not buying a kebab in daylight, despite how tempting it seems. I devour my snack in two mouthfuls and tell myself that will sober me up and give me another hour of drinking time. If I can manage another hour of drinking time that should allow just enough time for Jake to arrive as I'm leaving, he will convince me to stay out for a bit longer and it won't look like I was out waiting for him. It's a fool proof plan. What do I want to happen when this plan falls into action? I don't know. I still want Greg. It's just nice to be wanted and right now, I don't know if Greg wants sex, me, his wife or all of the above.

To my surprise Jake is already there when I arrive. That's early for him. When we were an item we wouldn't come out until about 8pm. I'm glad I saw him before he saw me. It gives me the opportunity to nip into the ladies and top up my makeup and check how tipsy I look. Once I am happy with what I have to work with I go to the bar, pretend I haven't seen him and order a drink. As if it couldn't get any easier, I feel a hand on the bottom of my back and he leans in and says hi.

'Hey! You're here. I didn't think you came out until later.'
'I was going to head back but I saw Dave and he kept me out.'
'Good old Dave. So that's you two out for the night then.'
'Yeah probably. What about you? Who are you here with?'
'Me? Oh um, my friends left and um, my other friend is coming out so I said I would wait for her here. She shouldn't be long.'

'Well come and join us then and wait for her to arrive.' He keeps his hand at the bottom of my back and escorts me to his table. I like his height next to me. I feel shielded and I feel like he is protecting me even though there is nothing to be protected from. Dave's face lights up when he sees me.

'Kate! My favourite of Jake's exes!'

'Dave! My favourite exes favourite friend!'

'I haven't seen you in ages. This is great. Tonight just got messy. I'll get the first round of jägerbombs.' Jake attempts to protest but Dave is already on his way to the bar. Jake liked his beer but he never liked having to handle me after too many. I would be the one who would end up on his friend's shoulders or in arm wrestling contests and although he didn't mind my 'fun' side, he didn't like it if it got too boisterous.

'Chill Jake. It's one round. I'm not staying out late anyway, I've been out all afternoon.'

'And that Kate, is what worries me.'

Of course it wasn't one jägerbomb. We all know that when someone says they are just having the one you can triple that. Three shots in and I am hogging the conversation, babbling on completely unaware of how drunk I am. Dave and Jake have been encouraging my drunken behaviour, it's good value after all. I am doing my best impression of Heather Small from The M People when I realise that they have stopped laughing and are looking over my shoulder. Someone is there. I look behind me tentatively to see that that person is Greg.

'I thought I might find you here. Do you want a lift home?'

'No fuck off. Give your wife a lift home.' I reply childishly.

'She is at home. You're not. Come on, you're wasted.'

'Look mate, she doesn't want to go' Jake chips in confidently.

Greg looks at Jake dismissively and then takes my arm. 'Kate, you're wrecked. Just let me see you home safely.'

I carefully rise and it becomes clear that I am in fact wasted. I can barely support myself and it hasn't gone unnoticed.

'Ssssee you guys later' I slur and allow myself to be escorted out by my wayward lover.

Kalopsia

Greg manhandles me into his car. Not deliberately but because my inebriated body is like a dead weight hanging off him. He straps me in and we drive off. The street lights are like strobe lights and my head is beginning to spin. I can't make sense out of what is happening and I instantly regret being this drunk in front of Greg. I have a horrible feeling that he is going to 'explain himself' and I won't remember a word of it in the morning.

'Fuck sake Kate. Did you really have to get yourself into this state? Is this what you do when I am not around? You should take better care of yourself.'

'Fuck you, Greg.'

'Look, I've said I am sorry about the holiday. I am not going to keep on apologising. You knew that the situation I am in is going to take time. It's just something we need to get through' he takes my hand in his, 'together. I can do it if you can. She knows we are over, it's for the kids. Please don't ruin something amazing over something... well something non-amazing. The marriage is dead. It'll be hard for me but we are doing it for the...'

'For the boys. I know Greg. So you keep fucking telling me.'

We pull up outside my flat and before he gets a chance to turn the engine off I am out of the car. I lean in and say, 'I hope your shitty holiday is shit.' I slam the door which doesn't work because I'm too drunk and so it just doesn't close properly and I leave it for him to deal with and stumble off. I look back and he is rubbing his forehead. Then, as if I haven't behaved like a child enough I give him the international hand sign of 'wanker' which I know I will regret tomorrow.

Chapter 19

The unnecessarily loud phone system is ringing letting me know that I have a visitor. I rub my eyes and immediately feel the pounding thud in my head. My mouth feels and tastes disgusting after smoking far too many cigarettes last night and it becomes clear that I am still pissed. Today is going to be a dark day. I peel myself out of my bed and gently place my feet on the floor. I am not ready to see anyone but the only way to shut up the intercom is to get up and grant access to whoever the sleep intruder is outside. I make my way to the door and look in the video cam. I can't see anyone but I can see a huge bunch of flowers. I mean, there is someone there but the bunch is so large it is blocking their head and body from view. I press the grey button to let them in and get a flicker of enjoyment from the shrill ringing that has stopped. However, the pounding in my head now sounds louder.

There is a gentle knocking at the door and I open it to a delivery man who looks as happy as Larry, as the saying goes. Who is Larry and why the fuck is he so happy? He probably doesn't consume his body weight in alcohol. Then there are flower delivery drivers. These people assume that women are delighted to receive flowers. Well, let me tell you, they are not always welcome. Surely, they should know that 95% of flowers bought are a form of apology. Don't ask me where I got my figures from, the School of Kate, if you will. I offer the man a false smile, accept the large and somewhat heavy bunch of flowers and close the door. No words were exchanged. All that happened is when he knocked on my door he was smiling, when he left he was not.

I take them through to the kitchen and dump them on the side. They are beautiful and I won't throw away good flowers, despite why I have received them. I am extremely glad that they come in water these days because I have zero energy to deal with them right now. I fish out the card and open the envelope.

'Kate, you are the one for me. The *only* one for me. Call me when you get these. I love you. Yours, G xxx'

Despite my head telling me to run a mile my heart flutters with glee and I know that once I have let him stew for a few hours, I will indeed call him.

Three hours later and Greg and I are in bed together. He arrived and as soon as I opened the door he took my head in his hands and I was too weak to say no. I love the way he kisses me with such passion and conviction. In between kisses he told me how sorry he was whilst undressing me. I don't want to lose him. I want to believe him. He makes me feel so good so there must be truth in that.

As we lay in each other's arms, he strokes my hair and I can't think of anything else apart from being here right in this moment with him. I feel warm, I feel safe and I feel happy and I feel a lot less hungover.

'Baby, I'm going to make it up to you. I'm going to prove to you it's about you and me.'

'Oh yeah? It would be quite easy to prove to me it's just you and me. Leave. Move out.'

'I will. I'm working on that. I promise, let me get Christmas out of the way but between now and Christmas I am going to show you a life that you've only ever dreamed of. Starting with... Miami.'

'What?'

'Well it's your birthday soon and I want to show you how special you are to me. I am going to take you to Miami. Just you and me for five days. What do you say?' He rolls on top of me and is an inch from my eyes.

'Seriously?' My heart begins to beat faster with excitement.

'Yes seriously.' He kisses my neck. 'So, is that a yes? Do you forgive me?' My heart was filled with glee until he said the word 'forgive' and suddenly I felt a pang of sadness as I am reminded of why he is doing this. My inner dialogue kicks in to quash my fears and tells me that I should give him a chance, that I will never know if I don't try. I can't tell if the inner dialogue is my voice of hope or despair talking.

'Yes, I would love to. You and me for five whole days, we've never had that before.'

'It will be amazing. We will do some cool things and I will get us a cool hotel on South Beach. You need to decide what you would like to do on the day of your birthday. Whatever you want, name it and we'll do it.'

As he begins to kiss me all over my mind is in turmoil. He wouldn't go to this effort for nothing. Yet he still lives with his wife. But, it's me he's taking away. If he was lying to me, she would ask questions about him being away for five days so it must be legitimate? They must be over and maybe she has moved on too. My thoughts and fears are hushed as Greg embraces my body for more passionate, make up sex.

Eventually we pull ourselves apart and Greg makes himself at home in the kitchen and starts cooking up a hangover cure. I lean against the doorframe in my Japanese silk kimono that he hates, and take in the picture. I love him. I am in love with this man and I won't give up on him. One day this will all be sorted and I've seen enough motivational posts on Facebook to know that good things never come easy so I am going to stand by my man whilst he deals with his separation. It's not ideal, I know that but we are so connected that I think this is the real deal and if I have to go through the rough stuff first to get to the happy ending then that is a fairy tale that I am happy with. I slope into the kitchen and put my arms around his waist.

'I do forgive you. I really do. I know things aren't easy but I want this and so I will wait for you.'

He turns around and gives me a kiss. 'And that is why I want you as my baby. I knew that you are emotionally mature enough to cope with this. That's one of the things that attracted me to you.' We kiss again. 'Now go and get in the shower. You smell of last night's booze and cigarettes.' He smacks my bum as I walk off and I suddenly feel hangover free.

At work, as the weeks pass, I have managed to ease into the position of secret girlfriend. I found it hard at first, I felt like everyone could tell and was paranoid about being *too friendly* with Greg when he was around. I voiced my concerns a few times but he was so relaxed and told me there was nothing to worry about. He said he actually liked it being a secret and said it was more fun that way. I don't think it's more fun, I want everyone to know about us but like he said, everyone will assume there has been an affair what with me only just breaking up with Tom and no one knowing him and Kirsty have split. I suppose it makes sense but I hate all the secrecy sometimes. What's crazy to me is no one even suspects. When Greg is in our office, he comes to my house for breakfast, we leave separately to go to work and we leave together at the end of each day and he comes back to mine. We are spending a good week once a month together and on top of that, once a week he books us in to a five star hotel and insists on me having as many spa treatments as I want. It's a thank you he says, for sticking by him in his difficult time. I meet him wherever he is working. He has flown me to Scotland and Dublin, we've stayed in Wales and all over England. He does what he can to make sure we get time together.

We have begun to get really close, sharing more and more of our secrets. I've told him about some bad things that happened in the past and he promises never to hurt me and tells me what a wonderful life we will have together. He has divulged more about Kirsty as time has gone on. He has told me about her lack of self-care and said she hasn't shaved downstairs in years. I asked him not to tell me that kind of stuff. I don't need to know that and I'd hate to think of someone talking about me in that way but for the record it's pretty tidy down there. You never know when a paramedic might need to save your life. Make sure your underwear matches and your bush is neat.

He told me her morning breath was horrific and how I am always so fresh. Is anyone fresh in the morning? It must be love if he thinks so. I told him not to tell me the personal stuff, it's not fair on her but some of the things he tells me, it's easy to see how the relationship broke down. He told me when his mother died she was cold and offered no comfort. He told me she used to brag to him and say he 'lucked out' when he met her and he said to me, *'who's laughing now'*. He told me how he loves how affectionate we are and how she hates people who put on PDA's. He said that they haven't had sex in years but how she happily spends three to five grand a month on his credit card and he doesn't know what on. I didn't believe someone could regularly spend that kind of money but he told me that she spent £600 on Adele tickets because she was stupid enough to go on the wrong website so I suppose repeated things like that could become quite costly.

One night we sat in bed drinking wine in the one of the Four Seasons hotels and he went into depth about how bad her post-natal depression had been hence why he is where he is now. He really opened up to me and I suddenly felt closer to him. He said it was so bad she would call him at work and say she had lost it and that he must return home immediately as she didn't trust herself with the baby. 'Can you imagine trying to run a multi-million pound business in the big city and having to run home to your nutty wife?' he said and went on to tell me this went on for three years and he stood by her side and so when his mother died and she couldn't even embrace him, that's what he knew it was over. She demanded that he had a vasectomy time and time again but he refused because in the back of his mind, he knew he would meet someone else. He stuck around knowing that one day, he would find the courage to leave. I was that courage, he told me.

After that evening, how could I not fall madly in love with this man? Even though he was flying away the next day for almost three weeks with the woman he had grown to dislike so much, it made sense. I knew I could make him happy and he could me, I just had to bide my time and not put too much pressure on him. I wasn't going to spend all his money, I have already worked longer in my life than she has. I wasn't going to be cold. I love affection and romance and he seems to like it too and I certainly wasn't going to take him for granted because

I knew if I loved him right, we could have the stuff that fairy tales are made of, which until recently, I didn't believe in.

The morning he left was brutal. We hugged, we cried and we kissed. The only thing that took the pain away was that he said this would be the last time he would ever do this and next time it would be me and him going away and building our future together. I waved him off and went to bed with a glass of wine at 11am. That was a first. I couldn't believe the pain I was feeling but I knew it would pay off in the end. I just had to get the next nineteen days out of the way. Nineteen days. As luck would have it, one of my best friends, Paulo, was working on board his flight. I had a word and told him to make sure Greg got a glass of champers on board. Paolo actually offered me a friends and family ticket to fly on that flight with him that night. Like a mentalist I considered it for a moment and I told Greg who also considered it and we hatched an insane plan to meet up in a hotel at various points across his holiday and the only thing that stopped it was that I wouldn't be able to get time off work with less than twenty-four hours' notice. It was mad, insatiable love talking. It was a stupid idea.

Just before they took off Greg sent me a whatsapp of him and Paulo, thanking me for the surprise. I replied 'xxxx' and buried my head into my pillow and cried.

Once I had finished feeling sorry for myself, it occurred to me that Paulo could be a really useful tool. He could tell me what they were like on the flight. Whether there was any obvious friction or whether they seemed like a happy family. I sent him a message, 'Text me as soon as you get this.' The next morning, Paulo replied 'What's up babe? Xxx'

'You met Greg and gave him the champers. He was travelling with his wife and kids. How did they seem?'

'Oh god darling, it was tragic. An outsider would not have said that was a happy marriage. He sat by the window with one kid and she was in the middle section with the other kid. No love there, you're fine babes. They didn't even speak to each other. That is one dead marriage. Now I'm off to see what Grindr has to offer me in Florida. Toodles xxx'

Relief. Sweet, sweet relief. I knew I was right to trust him. Well, between you and me I didn't but Paulo backed up Greg's story so things are looking good.

Shortly after I spoke to Paulo I got a text from Greg.

'Just landed. Missing you already. This is going to be hard for me too. Met Paulo, nice guy. Also, have you been in your bedside drawer? ;) xxxxx'

'Hey, this holiday of yours is going to drive me crazy. I know you will be busy but keep in touch when you can. Paulo is great, you can meet him properly when you get back. No, I haven't… going now…'

He is still online on Whatsapp.

I go into my bedroom knowing that obviously he left a present for me when he was here yesterday. I feel giddy with the romance behind it. I love presents. I love surprises. I love to know he is thinking of me. I open the drawer to find a Selfridges bag neatly tucked in there and then I look at my phone.

'Selfridges?!'

'Open it baby and be quick. I have to go in a minute xxxx' I open the bright yellow Selfridges bag to find a box inside. I can tell immediately it is a wrapped jewellery box. My heart begins to race. I gently pull away the paper and am holding the small, soft velvet, little black box in my hand. This is a ring box. I can't believe it. What has he bought. I prize it open and see a beautiful, diamond encrusted, platinum eternity band. I tease the ring out of its box and immediately put it on the third finger of my right hand. I quickly take a picture and send it to him with four love heart emojis.

'I can't believe you! When? Why? It's beautiful! I love it xxxx'

'You are beautiful and I love YOU. It's to say sorry about this trip and it's a promise ring. You are the woman I want to be with. This is the first ring you get from me xxxx'

I look at it in all its glistening glory. It has diamonds all the way around. Dirty diamonds, it has a dark grey look about it. It's different and I know he chose it because that's my style. He's messaged again;

Kalopsia

'Baby, I have got to go now. I love you. Don't give up on me. This time will pass and then I will be all yours. Love you more than words can say xxxx'

'I love you too, more than you know xxxx' he reads the message and just like that he is offline again.

I sit on the bed and stare at my new jewel. It really is beautiful and looks expensive. Knowing him it probably was. I wonder if I can find out how much it cost. Not because I need to know how much he spent but at the same time, if he has spent serious money then that would tell me how serious he is. I grab my laptop and begin investigating. After about ten minutes of trawling the jewellery section on the Selfridges website I find the ring. It cost him £1,000 exactly. I put my laptop down and stare at the wall in shock. *He must really like me. You don't just buy a fling a £1,000 ring to say sorry?*

I go and make a coffee and have a spring in my step without the caffeine hit. The more time passes the more I feel that this is the real deal. Greg and me all the way. I begin to picture our wedding after all he said this is the first ring. I picture us hosting dinner parties for our friends and the ladies commenting on my beautiful jewellery and Greg touching me at any opportunity. He would try to get past me in the kitchen, navigating his way around the island in the middle but not without sliding his hand along the bottom of my back. He would kiss my naked shoulder whilst I am at the sink. I am wearing a sleeveless dress by the way. For this made up scenario let's say it is a small black Karen Millen number. Sophisticated but sexy. His friends tell him to put me down and make jokes about how we are like love struck teenagers.

I awake from my daydream wondering how he knew what size of ring I needed? He must've looked through my jewellery without me knowing. I jump up and down with how lovely this feels and try to forget about the fact that he has just landed in America with his wife and children and is playing happy families. *Just hang on in there Kate, you'll get your man.*

I continue making a strong coffee and get ready to distract myself for day one of the awful separation.

Chapter 20

A week in to Greg's stupid holiday and I'm doing ok, not great, but ok. I have cried a few times at the thought of my man sharing a hotel room with his wife but thankfully it's a twin room, he told me. Still, I have driven myself to the point of despair imagining many scenarios of them rekindling their dying romance. One vision I had was that they were silly drunk and had crazy rampant sex, another vision was them sitting up late going over old memories and falling into each other's arms and having meaningful, soft sex, another vision was that this is all a lie and she has no idea and they are having normal sex. Every single scenario is as painful to think about as the other.

Thankfully, I don't need to worry. On the eighth day that they were all away I awoke to a video that Greg had sent of himself wanking. Although it was fairly graphic and didn't have the affect he was hoping for, it told me he can't be sleeping with her if he so desperately needed to wank and wanted me to see it. This is what I love about this man, he pulls me back into reality as quickly as my mind runs away with me. He has phoned me twice a day every day whilst he has been away. First thing in the morning and last thing at night, my time. We talk for an hour each time so I actually feel like I am getting to spend time with him. He even said to me that he sits in the bar in the evening to talk to me and the bartender had sussed him out. He said the bartender has seen how utterly miserable he is with his wife and how all he does is laugh and smile on the phone with me. He offers me this kind of information all the time. He is constantly reassuring me and it works.

One of the things he has been doing that I don't like is sending me family photos. It's weird but it makes me feel really uncomfortable. I just don't think I should be having that level of disclosure at this stage. Kirsty must be taking the photos and he is sending them to me. It doesn't feel right but I know he is trying to share with me so I have to be tactful about how I deal with it. That was until he sent me a picture of his youngest son who had made friends with a girl who looked about eight and she was wearing a bikini. That was too much and I told him. Firstly, I said that I didn't have the right to have access to the family album as it were and secondly, I don't agree with young children being sexualised so please don't send me any pictures of your children in a bikini, I don't like it. He replied immediately and said we were on the same page. He said the bikini was gross and that they'd had an argument about it. He said they shouldn't be taking pictures of children in swimwear but she thought it was cute that Henry had a girlfriend. He said he loved it how my parenting style matched his and how he knew I would make a fantastic mother one day. He didn't get the full message though because the next day he sent me a picture of his son in a wetsuit with the caption, 'Much better. I won the argument.' It's nice to be in touch but I don't need to know everything.

Later that week I caught up with my good friend Stacey. I invited her over for a take away and wine. More wine than take away. A girl's night in was just what was needed, so I thought.

Stacey does not approve of the Greg situation and we spent the whole evening talking about why it's not a good idea, according to her. She told me what I already knew but what she doesn't know is that I am already invested and too weak to break away. We discussed at length about how he shouldn't be pursuing a new relationship when he hasn't exited his previous one. She asked me to consider the fact that he is lying to me and isn't separating. She even suggested that I ask him if I can meet Kirsty, so that I know everything is above board. That simply isn't an option. That isn't the way he likes to deal with things. I can tell that he is a private person and there is no way he would want to mix both worlds when it isn't needed. I tried to tell Stacey that I would meet Kirsty when I meet the boys. Stacey urged me to call it off and said that it might prompt him to get his act together quickly and tried to reassure me that if we were meant to be together then we would be. I knew what she was saying was right but I felt powerless. I don't want to leave him. I believe him and I believe in us. All the things he says, the gifts he buys, the plans we make, surely that can't all be for nothing? He wouldn't make plans for the future if he didn't see a future? I told her about Miami and she said it sounded like he was trying to buy me. She said it was typical behaviour of a man who was having his cake and eating it. That would make him sick and he's not sick. He's a gentleman, he's loving, he's sweet, he's everything I have ever wanted. I don't expect anyone to understand but they will see. It will all work out in the end.

The evening progressed and I told her the conversation was getting a bit heavy. Between you and me I was close to tears because I missed him so much and I was trying to supress any suspicion from growing in my thoughts. I poured us some wine and it wasn't long before there were two empty bottles on the table and we were doing karaoke in our pyjamas. After singing Cyndi Lauper's 'Girls just wanna have fun' and falling into each other's arms laughing, Stacey took the conversation to a dark place again.

'Seriously Kate, what are you doing?'

'I know, I can't sing drunk or sober. It seemed like a good idea twenty minutes ago.'

'That's not what I meant and you know it. I'm worried about you. I think Greg is a bad move, especially after Tom. I can't help but think you were vulnerable and he knew it. He's playing you.'

'He is not playing me! I am a grown up and I can do what the hell I like.'

'I know, I know but look at it. You're almost thirty and you finally left dickhead Tom and have gone straight into another unsuitable relationship. I think you are going to get hurt.'

We sit in silence for a moment and I examine my wine glass with intent. I don't have anything to say. Her mind is made up and anything I say is going to sound defensive. I can't win.

'When you were still with Tom, you told me you wanted to run away and work in Barcelona for a year. You're not with Tom now so why don't you go and do it. Now is the time. Go to Barcelona whilst you are free.'

'I'm not free. I'm with Greg.'

'Kate. Greg is with Kirsty.' Stacey puts her hand on my arm and I try my damned hardest to stop the tears from rolling out and stop my chin from wobbling. I don't do a great job of it and we hug briefly before I laugh it off and Google 'Account Manager Jobs Barcelona.'

At the insistence of Stacey, I do a mass mail shot of my CV to companies in Barcelona and send my details to a few recruiters. After far too much wine, we finally head to bed knowing that the next day will be painful.

Trying to be productive at work in his absence was a struggle too. I think everyone thought I was ill or something and just ignored me. I was quiet, didn't laugh, didn't make conversation, didn't do the tea/coffee rounds. It's as if I wasn't really there. I knew I needed to be more careful. I couldn't let my colleagues notice my dramatic mood lift when Greg was next in but I was just so miserable without him. I would stare into his empty office, gaze over at his empty car parking space. I just wanted him to come back so that we could be together again. There was no doubt about it, this man was under my skin. Normally in relationships I have been the one who loved less but in this set up I think I love him more than he loves me. I feel like it's all out of my control. He mesmerises me. He captivates me. I want him and all his flaws. I once dumped someone for wearing a dirty jacket on a date and now look at me. This man is seriously flawed and yet I won't give up on him.

Over the course of the second week he is away, the phone calls continue and all of my fears and concerns melt away into nothing when we speak. It's as if soft, warm velvet is being poured into my ear when we talk. The molten lava of security enters in through my ear drum and slowly works its way into my body, warming me all over, easing any unpleasant thoughts, sealing any wounds. His voice is the elixir of happiness and contentment. He sends me heaps of love quotes he has found on line and he thinks about them. They aren't chosen at random, they are about distance, tough times, being reunited, making plans, good things are worth the wait. He knows the situation isn't ideal and he is rewarding me for putting up with him. He wouldn't do that if he didn't mean it. He wants what I want. He told me on the phone one evening that he only has one marriage left in him, that for him, I am his happy ending. He also told me he has been shopping. That tells me they really aren't spending a lot of time together. If you add up the two phone calls at an hour long each day, the numerous texts and now shopping for presents for me… they can barely be spending any time together at all. I have nothing to worry about and it will all come good, I can feel it.

Chapter 21

It's the night before Greg is due back, well actually, he will be on his flight now. I feel giddy. I feel tingly. I feel…happy. This trip has been worse than I thought it would be. I have been anxious, I have been depressed. I have been nervous. I have struggled to quieten my mind but I suppose it's all normal for a situation that isn't normal.

I run myself a steaming hot bath and I am gliding through my flat as if I am a ballerina instead of dragging my feet like heavy stones as I have been for the last three weeks. I simply cannot wait to see him. I light some candles whilst humming a love song. I never hum but I'm humming tonight. I pour myself a glass of red wine. I never really drank a lot of red wine before I met him but every time he visits he brings me a selection of wines and educates me on them. Tonight, I have an Argentinian Malbec and it's a very good one, so he told me.

He sent me a medley of love quotes on Whatsapp before he took off on the aeroplane. One read, 'one more sleep until I see my baby', another read 'You will never know how much I missed you', and another one said, 'It's always been you' and then he sent me a picture of a couple having sex against a wall and said that's what we would be doing in about eighteen hours.

I sank myself into the bath and suddenly felt sexy again. I took my time shaving my legs as if I were a vase about to be put out on display. I slowly made sure that every hair was carefully removed, no rushing and finding a whole strip I've missed later. I took my time. I wanted to be perfect for my imperfect man.

After I got out I lovingly applied body butter all over myself, yearning for his touch, knowing it would be soon. He always compliments me on how I take care of myself and no man wants to come home to a lazy woman. Men like to buy their women gifts and you don't need to buy them gifts back. They are visual creatures. Take pride in your appearance and that is the gift that they want. Never let your standards slip. Always shave. Always moisturise. Never have a chipped nail. Smell good. Have glossy hair but have bed hair. They don't like it pristine and poker straight. It must be something to do with reminding them of how you look once they have had their way with you. You are the present. That's what I've learned and it has been mainly Greg that has taught me that. He seems so appreciative that it makes me want to do it more. An old woman at a bus stop once told me, 'Keep their bellies full and their balls empty' and it struck a chord. They are animals and it is that simple but you have to make sure it's you that they want to empty their balls for.

After painting my toe nails a dark red, almost the same colour as my wine, I was ready for bed. I was shaven, exfoliated, moisturised and eager to see my beau. I went into my bedroom with a big grin on my face, knowing I would struggle to sleep tonight but for all the right reasons. I gently traced my fingers along the edge of my bed visualising me and him in it together tomorrow. I peeled back the blanket and lay my suddenly light body down.

I thought about what had been an extremely challenging, three weeks and how it was now almost over and I wouldn't have to suffer at Greg's marital globe-trotting hand again. From tomorrow onwards everything was going to get better. Soon he would be moving out and we could be together properly and in a few weeks from now we would be going on holiday together. Alone for five whole days. Away from prying eyes. Away from jilted exes and nosey colleagues. Just me and him having some fun in the sun.

I scrolled through all of our photos on Whatsapp and felt electric. I have never been so happy. He was everything I wanted. All of my friends said they couldn't see the attraction, they didn't think he was good looking and the common denominator was that he was 'punching above his weight'. That is an expression I have never liked. I am not with him for how he looks. I am with him because of who he is and who he is makes him attractive to me. He's sweet. He's generous. He's loving. He needs me. He needs to be reminded of what love is actually like. He needs to be appreciated. He's a geek. He is highly intelligent and I find it quite sexy. So what if I'm a sapiosexual? The world would be a better place if there were more of us around.

'Oh Kirsty, oh baby...' I can see him. His naked body on top of her and he is making love to her with the same amount of passion as he has when he makes love to me. His mouth is all over her chest and he's thrusting hard whilst calling out her name and calling her baby. I try to scream at him to stop but nothing comes out. I put my hands over my eyes but I can't block out the image. I might as well have been punched in the stomach and kicked to the ground because that's what it feels like, seeing them together like this. I begin to sob and yet I still can't scream at them to stop. I am just frozen to the spot, a spot that could be in hell.

I awake with a jolt. I feel my face and it is damp with tears. The dream was so vivid that is seems like it was real. I begin to cry consciously. I sob and I sob and I sob. This love affair is crippling me. The highs are like nothing I have ever experienced but so are the lows. He doesn't seem to understand that his words are like honey but his actions sting like a bee. *Why won't he just bloody end it now and leave her!* I punch my pillow in frustration and sigh. *You got yourself into this mess Kate. You knew what you were taking on.* It would be hopeless trying to get back to sleep now so I get up and make myself a chamomile tea in the hope that it will calm me down. Deep down I know that the image that woke me from my sleep will stay with me for quite some time.

As I make my tea in the dark, the microwave clock tells me it is 1:15am. I sigh again. I am wired. My mind is racing and he is coming to see me in about eight hours and I am going to look like shit.

I have started a diary. It's not a daily diary but I discovered one evening when I was particularly torn that writing down how I was feeling helped me to gain sense of the situation. Tonight was one of those nights where I was going to have to write this out otherwise my mind would not shut up. The book is stashed away at the back of a drawer. I don't have him down as the snooping type but I hide it just in case. If he read this book he would think that I don't trust him and he would probably think I am crazy. Sometimes this relationship makes me feel crazy. I have never felt so confused. Normally I have a strong sense of intuition but at the moment I can't tell what is intuition and what are insecurities.

That's why I keep this book. I write down everything he tells me. What he tells me about her, what he tells me about his day, his work, his childhood, his friends. Everything and anything. Then I write down how I feel and I look for any patterns. I am double checking to see if I am being sucked in but at the moment I believe him. Occasionally I am niggled by the thought that I am in love with him. Is the wool being pulled over my eyes because of my love for him? Will I look back on this one day, broken, and realise how obvious it was that he was lying the whole time? No, that can't be true. He's complicated, he's not an asshole.

I go through my messages and write them down in my diary. I write down the dream, sorry the nightmare that woke me. I write down every detail and then I write down why I might have dreamt that. I came to the conclusion that it is a buried fear that I am refusing to confront and so it is escaping through my dream mind. I don't want to confront it consciously. So far, he hasn't given me a reason not to trust him and if I start digging for evidence there will be no going back.

My chamomile tea is cold and untouched. I quickly knock it back and hide my diary away again. I do feel better for writing it all down but I know I still won't sleep well. I just need to have a clear head for when I see him tomorrow. I don't want him to know I have my worries. Never show weakness. The old British adage, stiff upper lip and all that.

I awake with an hour to get ready. I'm not great at rising but today is special. He's back and I can't wait to see him. I hop out of bed and look in the mirror. 'Great.' As expected, I have puffy eyes. My morning cup of hot lemon water should help that. I love it how he copies everything I do. Since being with me, he now drinks hot lemon water in the mornings. He even said one of his sons tried it too because he saw him doing it. I love being a positive influence in his life. What was once just part of my morning routine now brings a smile to my face knowing that we are gradually becoming one. Two people forging a path to be together.

I jump in the shower and sing along to my happy playlist on my phone. In less than an hour he is going to be here and all the misery from the last three weeks is washing away from my pores and down the drain in the shower. Just as I am wrapping my towel around me the door goes. *Shit, he's early.* I tiptoe to the door and look through the peephole. It's him and he's loaded with gifts. Before I can even open the door properly he plants his lips on mine, closing the door with his foot behind him. He dumps his bags on the floor and guides me towards the bedroom whilst never leaving my lips. He pushes me onto the bed whilst holding on to my towel so that I become completely exposed. He is frantically undoing his belt, he doesn't even take his trousers off. He just pulls them down enough to reveal his incredibly erect penis before lowering himself on to me.

I suppose you could say he was happy to see me.

Chapter 22

After rolling around in bed together and making everything right between us we uncoil our bodies and get up. Greg tells me to send an email in to work telling them I need to work from home. He isn't expected in today and he says that way, he doesn't expect me to get dressed today. I do it without hesitation. I am addicted to how much he wants me and needs me. We pick up exactly where we left off and it's like we have never been apart. It's so easy and it's so right. He's loving, he's insatiable, he's funny. He won't keep his hands off me. Even as I make us coffee, he scoops my hair away and kisses the back of my neck. I have to stop pouring the hot water because my knees are about to buckle. His kisses turn into sucking and before I know it his hands are inside my skimpy black satin gown and he's grabbing my breasts. It's clear we aren't having coffee just yet because Mr Owen is about to have his way with me against the countertop.

When Greg and I have finished what we started in the kitchen, we take our mugs through to the lounge. He tells me to make myself comfortable on the sofa and to close my eyes. I know he is going to get my presents.

'Hold out your hands but keep your eyes closed.' I hold out my hands like a giddy schoolgirl. Rope handles of a fancy cardboard carrier bag are placed in my palms. The bag feels heavy.

'Ok, you can open them now.'

Like most people I am not comfortable opening presents in front of an audience. I hate all eyes on me. The bag has been tied closed with a ribbon. I pull on one bit of it so that it all slips apart and I can feel Greg's eyes on me. There are several gifts in here.

'Oh wow. You shouldn't have! How many gifts are in here?'

'Not enough. Now open them.'

He has bought me a bottle of perfume, two pashminas, some jeans and two tops. At the bottom of the bag are two black jewellery boxes. I look up from the bag and meet his gaze.

'Come on, don't be shy. Open them.' Inside one is a beautiful necklace with a green sparkling gem stone. Inside the other is a matching dangling earring set. They are stunning.

'Once we went to a networking event together and you had your hair up. Have I ever told you how sexy your neck is? You should show it off more and wear this when you do.'

He joined me on the sofa and took the necklace. Once again, he scooped my hair away and delicately put the necklace on me with a couple of neck kisses in between.

Suddenly, and I don't know why, I pictured him with her. Instantly, my chin began to wobble and I felt a lump in my throat. I had to try my best to fight this. I didn't want him to know I was so insecure. Not after presenting me with all of these lovely gifts. It was no good. I let out a whimper despite my best efforts to contain it. Teetering on the edge of happiness was killing me.

'Kate?' he placed his hands on my shoulders and I buried my head in my hands.

'Kate? Babe, what's wrong? If you don't like it you only have to say,' he joked. I began to sob heavily. Greg sprung up from behind me and positioned himself on the floor in front of me. He was kneeling at my feet trying to take my hands away from my face before giving up and consoling me.

'Babe, I don't know what's wrong. Please calm down. Whatever it is, we can figure it out. Have you cheated on me?'

That statement was enough to give me a moment of calm.

'What? Have I cheated on you? Hell no! I can't do this Greg. I can't cope with it anymore. I have never had to share before and I don't want to. You said you were leaving and I need you to decide. I just can't keep this up.' I shocked myself by what I said. I did not see that courage coming.

'Oh baby.' He cuddled me tightly. 'You are not sharing me. I am yours. There is no question of that. The worst bit is done now. We just need to get Christmas out of the way and I am gone.' He continued to hug me whilst attempting to soothe me like a baby. 'Honestly Kate, please don't worry. I am leaving. You and I will be together. Don't these gifts show you that? I was on holiday with my family but I was shopping for you. I called you twice every day. I messaged you every day. I sent you a video of me wanking! I don't do stuff like that Kate. You have made me a new man. I feel alive. Don't give up. I just need you to be a little bit more patient and all will come good in the end. We are going to Miami in three weeks and I am going to show you the time of your life. It is going to be amazing. You'll see.'

We hugged tightly as I tried to regulate my breathing. I was so embarrassed I didn't want to look him in the eye. He must think I am a child. I need to be tougher than this. I need to show him I can handle it. I know how happy he makes me when we are together and in a few months, I will have that permanently.

We go back to bed, not for sex but to lie and sleep together. He spoons me and pulls me in tight. He strokes my hair and kisses my head and tells me again how much he loves me and that he is sorry for my pain. I've never met anyone who puts me back together so quickly after breaking me so easily.

Chapter 23

Three weeks have passed and now I am getting up early to leave for Miami with my lover. I have never been so excited. We have five unsolicited days together. We are meeting at the airport because he had business in London yesterday. Initially I was disappointed but then I realised I can get ready on my own schedule, make sure I look smoking hot and glide in to the airport with an air of calm around me. This was my opportunity to keep him waiting for once and I wanted to arrive and make sure he couldn't keep his hands off me.

I pranced about my home with music blaring and made myself a cafetiere of posh coffee because I was on holiday mode. I even poured it into one of my fancy coffee mugs that came with a saucer. I knew I was about to be treated like a princess for the next five days so why not start at home.

My female empowerment playlist was filling me with vigour for the day ahead and the eleven hour flight that awaited me. It wasn't intended to be a female empowerment playlist, it was just one day I noticed it was pretty cliché with all of the favourites for any woman lacking in confidence. It boasted Chaka Kahn 'I'm every woman' and 'Ain't nobody' etc. You get the drift.

After thinking I was a pop star in the shower and carrying on the music video audition into my bedroom whilst trying to find something to wear, I finally gave up the act when I couldn't decide what to wear.

Why did I care so much? How impressed did he need to be exactly? Why am I fighting for a man who tells me I am his?

I slump down on the bed and take a moment to feel sorry for myself. It occurs to me that maybe, just maybe, the driving force behind my excitement is not because I am going to Miami. Not because I am going to celebrate my birthday with the man I love. Not because of all the fun things we will do but the main reason behind my excitement is that we are going to be alone together. That's not right. In fact, it's sad. No one should be this excited about the prospect of being alone with their partner. Deep down I know this isn't right. The insecurities begin to creep in and I put my hands over my face and start kicking my legs as if I'm cycling just to shut them out. Knowing that this will never work I decide to have a cigarette and a glass of wine. I don't care if it's only 10:30am. I'm on holiday mode and the love of my life is a married fucking man and I think he's lying to me. I don't know how much longer I can keep up with this.

I smoke my cigarette quicker than a year eleven behind the bike shed who can hear the footsteps of the head of year coming and I drink my glass of wine quicker than a twelve year old at a wedding. I don't normally drink wine like that but I was having it for the buzz, not for class.

I finally decide on an outfit. Jeans with knee high hunting style boots, a sophisticated blouse and a tweed blazer. It looks like I've made an effort but I haven't. My favourite look. Natural make up applied, a mist of perfume sprayed, passport – check, dollars – check, plugs off – check – keys, phone charger, phone – check, check, check. Fuck it, I'm leaving now. If I have forgotten something I will have to buy it out there.

I arrive at Heathrow and Greg is waiting in clear view for me to see. My heart skips a beat as soon as I see him and I wonder if I should play it cool and glide towards him or run to him with open arms and plant my lips on his. Before I have time to decide, he nods his head in the direction he wants us to head and begins walking ahead of me. I can't lie, I am disappointed. I thought he would at least cuddle me and kiss me on the cheek. Anyway, no time for being a brat. We have to check in and get through security.

Throughout the process, Greg seems on edge. I know he is not relaxed at home but I hadn't expected him to be like this today. I get more and more pissed off with the situation and struggle to hide it. I know the airport is not the place for a 'strong word' so I have no option but to appear sulky. He knows I am pissed off and it seems as if he isn't that bothered about it. Once through security he continues to hurry me through the airport. I thought we would walk hand in hand, looking in the shops together, giggling and irritating everyone around us. I was clearly, very wrong. Greg has whisked us through the airport and I have teetered along behind him on my heels which are too high for the speed he wants me to walk. He takes us to the first-class lounge and the minute we pass the threshold he changes.

The immaculate waitress leads us to a table but Greg leans forward and whispers in her ear. She smiles and her face lights up and I feel a pang of jealousy. This guy is seriously starting to piss me off which does not bode well for a five-day trip together. I take my jacket off and prepare to walk to one of the two seated glass tables when the oriental beauty starts to panic and takes my coat from me. She apologises profusely and leads us away from the tables and down a seductively lit passage way and into our own private room. The room is dark and has leather sofas but more importantly, a bottle of Bollinger chilling in a bucket of ice. There is a card next to it and I pick it up. It reads, 'Happy Birthday, Kate xxxx'

I didn't even notice the waitress leave the room because Greg has taken me into his arms and begins kissing me heavily and undoing my blouse.

After a boozy wait for our flight we are finally boarding and I am so excited. I still can't believe Greg is whisking me away on holiday for my 30th. Just the two of us for five whole days. No having to hide, no walking separately. We can hold hands, we can kiss at a bar over a cocktail, we can be just what we are, two lovers who are crazy about each other. I try to take his hand as we board the plane and he shakes it

Kalopsia

off to retrieve his boarding pass. Oh well, plenty of time for that when we take off. We find our seats and Greg has to go to the bathroom. He eventually returns when the plane is boarded and getting ready for take-off. He gets in to his seat next to mine and appears apprehensive.

'Hey, relax. It's just you and me now and that makes me very happy.' I stroke his hand and peck him on the mouth. He isn't one for public displays of affection but I will be changing that when we are in Miami.

'Well hopefully you get a seat like this on the way back.'

'What do you mean?'

'Well we are at the front so we have extra leg room. You'll want that on the way back so that you can try and sleep.'

'Why do you keep saying *you* and not *us*?'

'I'm not flying back with you. I have to work.'

A surge of heat rushes to my head, my mouth fills with saliva and my palms become clammy. 'What do you mean you have to work and why is this the first I am hearing about it?'

'Kate, relax. You're a big girl, you'll be fine. I have to work. Trips like this won't pay for themselves. There is a seminar that I am speaking at after you have left so I'm staying on for a couple of days.'

I look down into my lap trying to digest what I am hearing. Greg takes my hand in his.

'You're not seriously sulking? Is there no pleasing you? I'm taking you away for five days, on a no expense spared trip. I thought you'd be pleased.'

'I am pleased, I just didn't realise that was the plan. You never said.' My insecurities are running wild but I remind myself to be grateful and to be cool. 'It's fine, I just wished you had said. Of course, I can come back alone.' He kisses me on the lips, let's go of my hand and puts his eye mask on. I know he is spoiling me but yet, I feel so disappointed. Where is the stewardess, I need a gin.

Chapter 24

Greg eventually wakes from his seemingly guilt free slumber and we enjoy a few in flight drinks together and begin to get back into the holiday spirit. The several gins that I had have pulled me out of my sulky behaviour and whilst he slept I told myself how grown up this was. I was travelling to the states with my high-flying partner and we were one of those couples where I am so laid back that I travel home alone to let him get on with business. I convince myself that this is all ok and that if I want to be with him, I have to accept that business is important to him. It's a small price to pay for the man of my dreams.

Once we land and the seat belt signs are off, Greg immediately gets his phone out and becomes engrossed in emails and messages. I really hope this isn't a sign of things to come. I have got my head around coming home alone but I don't want to be a mobile phone widow as well. He must have detected my mood because he puts it away and pulls me into his mouth by the chin. We have a sneaky kiss and then he gets our bags down from the overhead locker. He signals for me to go first and as I squeeze past him he smacks my bottom and reaches further under to stroke me. It's clear what's on his mind again.

Inside the airport Greg becomes engrossed in his mobile again whilst ushering me on through customs. I'm too excited to care. So what if he needs to check his work emails, better that he does them now than when we get to the hotel.

Naturally we are buzzing out of the airport, into the taxi and on our way to the hotel but it isn't long before the tiredness kicks in. As we pull up outside our five-star home on Collins Avenue, Miami, I almost have to pinch myself. This is the kind of thing that dreams are made of for a girl like me. Add to that, the rush of being with my boss. I still get a kick out of that. The hotel staff open our cab doors and appear to be our new best friends. The humidity is unbelievable and I feel my clothes turn to cling film immediately. Within seconds I am in the very cool and very soothing grand foyer of our hotel and it strikes me that despite how vast the entrance is, I am hit by a fog of white lily perfume. The atmosphere is electric and I could almost stand here and just soak up the cacophony of the leavers and joiners.

Greg says he will check us in and tells me to wait and the bar. He says to order whatever I want but suggests that we should probably have champagne. I'm not one to argue. I make my way over to the bar and am greeted by the bartender who again, has the skill of making me his new best friend down to an art. He has a Latino complexion and dazzling white teeth and is dressed in white. All the staff are dressed in white and it gives me the impression of heaven on earth. I can't understand how these people can live and work in this climate. I don't let it worry me too much though. My concern for their hair going frizzy is quickly forgotten as the ice bucket with a bottle of Bollinger is presented to me. The bartender pours me a glass and as I wait for Greg, I take a sip and absorb my surroundings.

The hotel furnishings are made of wood and linen and have a very natural feel. Adjacent to the bar area is a healthy juice and breakfast bar. It seems so clinical yet so fabulous. It's as if they have brought the spa into the main lobby of the hotel.

Greg joins me with a big grin on his face. He pulls out the bar stool next to me and pours himself a glass of bubbly. Before he drinks it, he pulls me in and kisses me hard on the lips and then embraces my whole body in a way that I was expecting when I arrived at Heathrow.

'I'm sorry baby. I just don't relax that well with travelling but we are here now and I've got you all to myself.'

He places his hand on my knee and rubs my leg dangerously close to my groin.

'Stop it you. We are in a public place.' I giggle like a little girl.

'I can't resist you. Come on, let's take this up to our room.'

As usual, I do not protest.

Once in the lift, Greg begins to devour me as if he hasn't eaten in days. His hands are everywhere and so is his mouth. I get the feeling if the lift was never ending we would go the whole way. The lift dings like a doorbell and the doors open whilst we are still heavy petting. A couple who are not quite as in love as we are, are waiting to get in and appear to be quite put out by our display of affection. Well, she does. He looks jealous.

Greg leads the way to our room and opens the door to what I can only describe as a slice of paradise. Again, the room is furnished in a natural wood and white linen finish. The window, as promised, gives us an amazing view right onto South Beach. The bed is huge and the lighting, whether deliberate or not, is seductive. The bathroom has a glass wall revealing the whole shower area to the bedroom. It's a good job we are not shy. Our bags are already here and I approach mine to begin unpacking.

'What are you doing?' Greg asks in between kissing my neck.

'I was just going to get organised.'

'You can't tell me that's the first thing that you want to do?'

'I am at your mercy, Greg. I can't believe you have done this for us. This place is magical.'

He doesn't say another word, instead, tantalisingly begins removing my clothes.

Once naked he pushes me onto the bed. He grabs his phone and positions it on the TV unit so it is facing us directly.

'You don't mind, do you? I want these memories to last forever.' I don't object. What's a video between two lovers. I wouldn't mind keeping those memories either. I don't know if it was the excitement of being away together or knowing we had each other to ourselves but the sex was passionate, explosive and ferocious. We almost couldn't get enough of each other. He pulled my hair and I scratched his back until we both climaxed together in a hot, humid mess.

After walking Collins Avenue that evening trying to find the best restaurant to try to stay awake in, we finally settled on one after walking past it three times. We were both fighting the jet lag but determined to stay up as long as possible in Miami time. We passed several fancy eateries and yet ended up in an edgy Mexican bar. We were in no fit state to care anymore, I used the classic traveller theory of picking somewhere that was busy. Once inside we had decided it was the right place because the menu featured a Kate Quesadilla. It was meant to be, at least that is what we told ourselves. We managed one drink and a few mouthfuls before admitting defeat and dragging our very tired bodies back to our luxurious, spa smelling hotel.

The next morning was skydive day and I am not ashamed to admit that I was feeling incredible queasy. Not even that first morning waking up together and tumbling in the sheets was enough to distract me as the event drew nearer.

I am afraid but not afraid to back out. I am committed. I am doing this. I am thirty tomorrow and I have developed a ridiculous fear of heights that can only be conquered by facing my fear from as high as I can go. It's a nervous excitement. Greg went down to the healthy breakfast bar and returned with a green smoothie each and a bagel. I couldn't eat it. Not because it was too healthy but because my stomach was on lockdown. I take in the view of South Beach from our balcony and try to adjust to the humidity. Greg can't bear it and is trying to keep cool in our air-conditioned boudoir. We are just milling around passing the time before we take the literal plunge. Before I know it, it's time to go.

We wait in the foyer for a cab and the incredibly friendly staff are more excited about our day than I am clearly. They can't believe we are going for a skydive together and they all egg us on as we get into our awaiting carriage and tell us they can't wait for us to get back. I give a sheepish smile with a gulp.

Greg being the wonderful man that he is can tell how nervous I am and talks to me about any old nonsense the whole way knowing full well that I am not listening to him. I am taking in the sights of Miami out of the window wondering if these will be the last images I ever see. The way I see it, if I die, it's going to be quick and if I die, I won't be alone because my experienced tandem sky diving instructor is going down with me.

We eventually arrive at the centre and by now I enter a stage of calm. I have given up the fight with fear and am ready to accept what happens to me. We are both handed a booklet to sign. A booklet! There are way more pages that require signatures than I expected and I don't even read what I am signing. If I do then I won't do it. That's a lie, I saw one page said something about it is not the instructors fault if he is under the influence of drugs and alcohol and an accident happens. That's when I decided to stop reading and just go for it. The next stage of the induction torture was being made to watch a video which basically reiterated the risks for twenty minutes but was wrapped up with, 'have a great flight' at the end. Cue more gulping from me.

As all of this was going on, various other nutters were getting ready to take the jump and reassuringly looked equally as sick as I felt. However, they would disappear outside and about forty minutes later they would re-enter the building looking like they had survived a hurricane but were totally buzzing.

Next, we were called in to the kit room to get ready. *Oh my god, this is really happening.* Greg is relaxed as usual. This was his second time so he was pretty calm. We don what I can only compare something similar to a gimp suit and practice sitting on the floor. Just as I tuck myself in between Greg's legs and he squeezes my waist to bolster my spirits our names are called out of the tannoy system. *This is it.*

By this point I have freaked myself out so much that I am ready to enjoy the experience just in time. We get out on to the forecourt and our extremely enthusiastic instructor makes a video of us before we board. He's throwing high five's around like he's stepped back into the nineties but he doesn't look like he's seen death and that offers me some comfort.

We board the tiny aeroplane and something that had never crossed my mind was how we would sit. I was first on to the plane and I had to sit on the floor with my back to the pilot. Greg was adjacent to me and immediately took my hand once we were strapped in. The door was closed and this was really about to happen. There was no backing out now, unless I refuse to jump. I'm not going to be that girl. We start to lift into the sky and I find it really weird watching the ground grow further away from me from this angle. I have only faced forward on an aeroplane before so sitting back against the pilot's seat and getting a view of the ground from this angle is slightly unnerving. I keep a close eye on my Altimeter. We are jumping from thirteen thousand five hundred feet. As I observe how tiny the ground looks I think we must be that high by now. My Altimeter says we are at nine thousand feet. Gulp.

That's it. We hit the thirteen thousand five hundred feet mark and the door gets thrown open. I don't know why but I expected a kind of vacuum sensation and that I would have to cling on for dear life but that didn't happen. It was just blustery and noisy. What freaked me out the most is that once the door was open and we were all about to jump, the instructors all give each other the ok signal and fist punch each other. *Not so fucking jovial now Mr Cameraman are you.* My instructor pretty much shunts me forward. I guess they have to do it in that way or people might mess about. I let go of Greg's hand and we kiss each other hard.

I have to make my way to the lip of the gaping hole in the plane on my knees with my instructor strapped on behind me. My heart is racing like it could burst out of my chest and my stomach keeps flipping like I am driving over a brook bridge quickly. I make my way to the exit and feel the air pummelling my face. I don't like being on my knees of an aeroplane door that is open thirteen thousand and five hundred feet up in the sky. I cross my arms across my chest as instructed in the training room and look up at the sky.

'One! Two!' Shove.

We are out of the plane and descending rapidly. The air is beating so hard against my face I can't breathe. I unfold my arms and stretch them out as far as I can. This is fantastic! I don't know what my legs are doing and I don't care. Who the fuck actually remembers what to do for the first time. My instructor symbols ok in front of my face and I signal back. This is incredible. Even if the parachute fails and I die in a few minutes time, this surge of adrenalin is the most epic sensation I have ever experienced. It is like an out of body experience. The photographer is in my face trying to get me to smile for a photo. I defy anyone to smile normally in that situation. I can only assume by the flapping sensation that my face will look like I have had a dramatic weight loss in the pictures. Suddenly I am jolted sharply underneath my arms and the parachute is up. Thank fuck for that.

The intense adrenalin subsides and is instantly replaced with tranquillity. We are gently making our way back down to earth and I have never felt so blown away, pardon the pun, in my whole life. I am even allowed to take the controls and steer us for a short while. I cannot believe I am here, skydiving down over the everglades. This is a birthday I will never ever forget. We gently float back down to land and Greg is already there waiting for me. It then occurs to me that I have to remember how to land. In the end, I put my legs out horizontally and hope for the best. It wasn't the prettiest of landings but who cares. I just skydived! I roll around in the grass in all my adrenalin fuelled glory and laugh. I laugh and I laugh some more. Greg comes over and gives me a hand to hoist myself up. I collapse my whole being into him like the most grateful girl in the world. That is an experience I will never forget. Could never forget!

'Amazing, isn't it?' He says tucking my flyway hair behind my ears.

'Oh my god, soo amazing! That was literally the best thing I have ever done.'

He looks at me puzzled. 'Not the *best* thing you have ever done?'

'Well no, that would be you but this is definitely second…and it lasted longer.'

He smacks my bum and we walk to the waiting mini bus hand in hand.

The rest of the day goes by in a state of post skydive euphoria. The cab on the way back into Miami is ten times louder than the cab on the way in. I am completely stoked and can't stop talking about what a fantastic experience we had. Greg melted my heart by saying how scared he was watching me fall out of a plane in front of him. We get the cab to take us to a shopping mall. Greg's idea, not mine but I am as agreeable as ever. As we approach the drop off zone, Florida does not disappoint with its reputation and the heavens open in spectacular fashion. We dart inside and make our way to the food area.

After this morning's stomach lock down, I am now famished. We get a table for two in a typical American diner bar and without messing around I order a double cheeseburger with fries, of course, and after a bit of confusion I successfully order a cider. It would seem that the UK is the only cider mad country. Over lunch I continue to run my mouth off like I am on a timer about how mind blowing the sky dive was and Greg just lets me talk and smiles at me. I think he feels pretty pleased with himself. My burger and chips are devoured in no time at all and we settle the bill and go shopping.

'We can go anywhere you like. You need to have something to open on your birthday tomorrow.'

'No way. You have done enough! This trip! The skydive! We haven't even been here twenty-four hours and already it tops any holiday I have ever had.'

'But it is still your birthday tomorrow and you need something to open. Come on, let's go in here.' He takes me by the hand and leads me into Tommy Hilfiger. He instructs me to pick something and says that he is going to browse the men's section.

I am not comfortable telling someone what to spend on me. If someone wants to buy me something that's fine but I have never been ok with the 'can I have this?'. It's just not me. After pretending to browse for ten minutes I go to look for him and tell him there is nothing I like. I zig zag through the men's department and he isn't there. I hesitate and think about returning to the women's section but I don't want to so I go looking for the ever evasive, Greg. There is a glass wall towards the back of the store separating the children's section from the adult's section. I spot Greg sitting on a faux leather pouf near the children's footwear. He is on his phone and is rubbing his temple with his spare hand. I pause and then quickly turn on my heels before he has seen me. *It could be a work call? It could be anyone? What does it matter?* I return to the women's department and knowing that he won't take no for an answer, I start seriously looking for something he can buy me. I'm browsing the bags when he comes up behind me, places his hands on my hips and kisses my neck.

'I like it. Do you want it?' I'm staring into space, not at the bag but I find myself agreeing.

'Do you like it? Can you see me with it?'

'Yes, it classy, like you. Have it. Pick something else too. What about a top?'

'No way. This is enough. Thank you. What about you, did you see anything you like?'

'Nah, not really.'

'Oh, come on! It can't be all about me. You deserve a treat too. Let's look together.' I take him by the hand and head over to the men's department. Straight away I spot a black sailing style jacket. It has Tommy Hilfiger emblazoned around the back of the collar but it still manages to appear sharp and stylish.

'What about this? This would really suit you. Try it on!' Greg begins feeding his arms through and I can see he likes it.

'You've got a good eye, Kate. I really like this.' He checks himself out in the mirror and I can see he is pleased.

'You look great. Get it.'

'Ok. I will.'

'Did you not see it before?'

'No. I must have walked past it.'

Yeah. Something like that, eh Greg. Let it go, Kate. Stop being such a spoilt bitch.

Kalopsia

Shopping purchased and back in the cab we are heading for home. Our temporary home overlooking South Beach. Our lovers' nest. Our little slice of heaven.

Miami weather is crazy. As we drive over the bridge away from the city and towards the beach, we leave the Armageddon-esque storm and drive into the blistering sunshine. We agree to dump our bags, don our swimwear and head for the roof-top pool for a spot of sunbathing and a cocktail. After the day we've had, it's the least we deserve.

Chapter 25

It's the morning of my birthday. Thirty years old. Wow. The bright Miami sunshine is peaking through our floor length linen curtains. I take in my surroundings with only one eye open. It's all I can manage first thing. I look round to see my lover is still in his deep slumber.

There is a bottle of Malbec with a small glass left in it on the coffee table. Two wine glasses next to it that are still full. A small tray of Café Crème cigars. A stocking here. Another stocking over there. A stiletto in one corner and the other one across the room. My dress is draped on the back of the sofa. My clutch bag is on the floor with the flap open and change strewn across the floor. I smile and remember how we raced back to our room with our bottle of wine but barely touched it before falling into each other's arms. I closed my eyes and cast my mind back to the night before. The dim lighting. The drunken passion. I could see myself lying on the sofa with my back arched, Greg's hands holding me whilst French kissing my breasts.

I kiss him on the cheek to gently wake him and he slides his hand onto me and squeezes my naked buttock.

'Coffee?' I whisper gently to him.

'Yes please.' He rolls onto his front and buries his head into his pillow. I peel back the light covers and get out of bed and start preparing the coffees. I am in my own world when I realise he has been staring at me.

'I love your confidence.'

'What?'

'The way you walk around naked without a care in the world.'

'Well, why wouldn't I? You've seen it all in all its glory.'

'And bloody glorious it is.'

I carefully carry our two coffees over to the bed and climb back in. He quickly springs up so that he is on top of me. He is rock hard and without waiting, he enters me and begins to thrust hard. I love the spontaneity, the passion, the desire he has for me. I feel weak and I am happy to lie there and take him in all *his* morning glory. It doesn't take long but I don't always need long. The mad sexual frenzy was enough to satisfy us both.

As we lie there, me in his arms, he traces his fingers all over my body.

'Well, Birthday Girl. What do you want to do today?'

'I would like to start with champagne. Then perhaps hire some bikes and go for a cycle along South Beach. After that, come back here for a dip in the pool and a spot of sunbathing. Then, after that, back to our room where we will make love again and get ready to go out for dinner.'

'That sounds like a bloody fantastic plan.' He plants a heavy kiss on my mouth and then pushes me out of bed.

'Go and get showered and dressed then and let the birthday celebrations commence.

Once ready, we head downstairs to the what is a fancy restaurant area at night but doubles up as a fresh, summer style beach bar during the day. The waitress takes our room number and shows us to our table. Greg asks for champagne to be brought to the table immediately. As she goes to get our drinks, Greg says he needs to go to the loo and leaves me at the table. I didn't mind for the first five minutes. I was only slightly confused after ten minutes. Once twenty minutes had passed I was getting pretty pissed off as I waited to toast my lover on my birthday. My gut was turning in knots. Something told me he was not in the loo. I tapped my fingers impatiently on the table and watched the twenty-fifth minute pass by. *What the fuck is he doing?*

Then in a moment of madness or genius, I'm not sure which, I decide to call him. Not as me but as a private caller. Maybe I am mad but my suspicions were correct. User busy. *Could be work, but I don't care. We are supposed to be on holiday and it's my birthday! Don't be a spoilt bitch Kate.*

Fighting the fiercely strong desire to slip in to a full-on sulk, I use my phone to distract me. I start mindlessly scrolling through my emails when one catches my eye. *Invitation for Skype Interview – Jones & Lunter LLP.* My heart skips a beat and I am immediately surprised by how excited I feel about this. I open the email;

'Dear Kate,

We were impressed by your recent application for an account manager position in our Barcelona office and would like to invite you for an initial Skype interview. We are currently hosting these calls on Thursday and Friday of next week. Are either of these days suitable for you?

Regards,
Maria Gonzalez
PA to Head of HR'

I lean back in my chair with a smile on my face. Life is good. Here I am in a five-star hotel looking out of a huge window on to Collins Avenue. It's my thirtieth birthday. Yesterday I did a skydive. Today I have already had two orgasms and have been invited to an interview for my dream job in my favourite European city and now I am downing this glass of champagne and it's only 10:30am. My nose fizzes as I gulp down my bubbles. I feel warm and know I will feel giddy any minute soon which is why I did it.

I feel a hand squeeze my shoulder and Greg has appeared forty minutes later. If I hadn't have seen that email I would have been somewhat incensed. I know I can't prove it but I am fairly confident that he did not go to the toilet but actually went to call home.

'Where's your champers?'

'It arrived forty minutes ago.'

'You drank it without me? It's polite to toast. I can't believe you didn't wait for me.' He is being serious which pisses me off even more.

'I did wait. I waited for thirty-five minutes, actually.'

'I have never been thirty-five minutes.'

'No. You were forty minutes. I drank the glass five minutes ago.' I wanted to tell him to check his call list if he didn't believe me. 'Anyway, I didn't realise I was restricted to one glass. It's pretty traumatic leaving your twenties. I should at least be allowed two.' He beckons the waitress over and orders me one glass and I note that he isn't going to have a second. I think he is genuinely put out that I didn't wait for him. *Sorry your lordship. I'm guessing Kirsty bows down to you. Well I am not Kirsty.*

I put my annoyance behind me and was determined to enjoy the day. We took a bike ride along the beach as I had suggested. The humidity was suffocating but not as much as my thoughts were crippling me about how this relationship would pan out. Once back at the hotel we changed into our swimwear and went to the rooftop pool. What I thought would be an afternoon of fun was an afternoon of Greg sleeping in the sun and me growing increasingly frustrated. I made my way over to the bar. A rather dashing man of dark mocha skin, dazzling white teeth and much more my age greeted me.

'Hey senorita, what can I get you?'

'I don't know. What would you recommend for a birthday drink?'

'It's your birthday? Well how about a cool, refreshing mojito on me.'

'That sounds perfect and I'll have a shot with it.'

'You're really going for it huh? So, a man should never ask but, how old?'

'It's my thirtieth.'

'Well that definitely deserves a shot. What about him?' He nodded in Greg's direction.

'Does he look like he needs a drink to you?' I said with disappointment on my face and in my voice.

'Well, if you will date an older man. I'm not surprised he can't keep up. An attractive woman like you must be tiring him out. Lucky guy.'

I gave a half smile and knocked back my shot. We were both thinking along the same lines but before he had the chance to say anything else I took my complimentary cocktail and made my way over to my quiet sun lounger. The more time I spent with Greg, the more alone I felt.

Later that evening we went out for a suave birthday dinner. The restaurant was very swish and we both looked the part but something had changed. I would be flying home in a couple of days, alone, and that's not how I imagined the trip being. I tried my very best to ignore my feelings but I couldn't and it was clear. I drank too much with dinner and all I wanted to do was go back to the hotel, crawl into bed and go to sleep and so that is what we did. I think Greg thought I was being a spoilt brat and I thought he was unable to see things from my point of view.

It was the morning of the end of my trip. The last couple of days had been spent sunbathing, having sex and drinking cocktails. Greg had stopped giving his phone so much attention and we actually relaxed and behaved like a couple. We giggled, we messed about like kids and we had fun. I got a taste of what we could be and now it was time to tear it all apart again.

As soon as the burning Florida sun woke me I could feel a lump in my throat. I wanted to cry. I wanted to bawl my eyes out and scream that none of this was ok. I got out of bed without waking Greg and went straight for the shower instead of making us a coffee first. For the first time on this trip, I was not happy about the glass wall between the bathroom and the bedroom. I turned my back to the glass and sobbed in the steam. If I could do this quietly and get it out of my system then Greg would never need to know and I could put a brave face on it for our last day together before my evening flight home.

I came out and Greg was up and packing.

'You ok?' He touched my arm as I walked past him refusing to make eye contact.

'Yeah.'

'Are you sure?'

'Mmm hmm.' I pulled my dresses out of the wardrobe and began to follow suit. The lump had not gone and I was fighting desperately to keep the tears at bay. Greg came up behind, put his arms around me and kissed my neck. That was it. I was gone. I turned into him and sobbed heavily on his shoulder.

'Shhh. Shhh.' He stroked my head delicately and pulled me onto the bed. I cried and I cried some more. 'Baby, what is this about?'

'I'm sorry. I tried really hard to contain this. I just. Uuurgh! I just hate it that I am going home without you. It's bad enough going home to separate houses but leaving you here just feels awful.'

Greg rubbed my back and repeatedly placed little tiny kisses on my temple. 'I'm sorry baby. I should've told you before we came. I just didn't think it would be this big a deal to you.' That annoyed me.

'Well I'm sorry this doesn't bother you as much as it bothers me. I can't keep doing this in secret. It isn't right. It's killing me. I should never have got involved with you until you moved out. We don't get proper time together like an actual couple.'

'Well, maybe I can do something about that in the short term. I've had an email this morning about a trip to Boston. Want to come?'

'Another business trip?'

'Well, yes, but I am being honest and upfront about it. I would only have to work for one day and one evening and the rest of the time we could spend together. Come on, say you'll come with me?'

'When is it?'

'December.'

'How long would we go for?'

'How does five days sound? We fly out together and fly home together and I will come back with you that night. Then, Christmas will be around the corner and I will move out as I have always said I would.'

Normally when a boyfriend says they are taking you away it would make you jump for joy. I was half jumping for joy but I was half disappointed that this was another business trip where I would be tagging along. Still, he was trying and that made me happy.

'I'd like that a lot.' This was progress and I was excited about it and I was sure that excitement would grow once I got over my tears. It took the edge over flying home alone tonight at least.

'Thanks Greg and I'm sorry for being a brat. I just want this, I want us so much.' I sat on his lap and he squeezed me hard. I began to cry again but more surprisingly, so did he.

After a final tumble in the sheets and my second shower that morning, we were packed and ready to check out.

'Are you asking for a late check out so we can get our bags later.'

'No, I'm going in an hour. Do you want me to ask for you?' My heart sank yet again. He wasn't with me for the day and he had failed to tell me that as well.

'Ah. I see. So…' Greg grabbed my face in his hands and kissed me. I reluctantly kissed him back.

'Baby, the other guys will be arriving soon. It was odd enough that I didn't travel out with them. I told them I was visiting a friend in Vermont. I can't stay with you today. Let's speak to reception, see if you can use the roof top pool and whatever you want, just tell them to charge it to the room. Ok?' I was staring down at the ground whilst examining my fingernails. 'Baby, we've got Boston to look forward to! I'll book the flights today and send you a screenshot. That will give you something to keep focused on. We are almost there. We knew this wouldn't be easy. Just hang on in there. For me. Ok?'

I nod half-heartedly and he kisses my forehead and smacks my bum.

'Come on, let's go and have one last glass of champers together.'

Chapter 26

We had a glass of champers as suggested but Greg knocked it back, got an Uber and was gone, just like that. It seemed to me that he was devoid of empathy at times. One minute he made me feel like the only girl in the world and the next, it was almost like I didn't exist. I told myself I was being over emotional and that everything would look better tomorrow.

I decided not to go to the roof top pool. For the sake of a couple of hours, I couldn't be bothered with the rigmarole of wet hair, changing in the toilets and fishing clean clothes out of my case. I decided that sitting around and having a good sulk was much easier and more appealing. A decision I would more than likely regret later but hey, I'm all for living in the moment and in this moment, I am pretty pissed off.

I went and took my drink and sat outside the front of the hotel underneath the umbrella's. It wasn't long before a rather tanned, overweight and over confident man came and sat opposite me. We exchanged the obligatory glances, a half smile each and I was hoping he would fuck off until he pulled out a packet of cigarettes from his shirt pocket. Suddenly he seemed a lot more interesting.

'Want one?' I must've been staring more than I had realised, fantasising about how lovely the sweet deathly nectar of nicotine would be right now in my current stress zone.

'No thanks. Oh, fuck it. Yes please.'

'That's some colourful language you got there, lady. You know it's not attractive for a lady to speak like that.'

'Well, I'm not attractive so who fucking cares.'

'Ooosh. You need this cigarette don't you. Here you go.' He passes me the packet with a tip hanging out for my easy retrieval and passes me his lighter. 'So, a young lady sitting on her own outside a hotel, swearing like a banshee and taking cigarettes from a stranger. Doesn't look good. Where is he? What did he do?'

I smirk and look away.

'Sorry, none of my business but you did take one of my cigarettes so you can't blame an old cat for being curious.'

I blow the smoke away from me petulantly but as the nicotine rushes through my body I unfold my arms and decide to relax.

'He's gone to another part of the city for a business trip and left me to fly home alone.'

'Doesn't sound too bad to me. He's working and you got a holiday out of it. What's so bad about that.'

I notice the sweat taking over his shirt and it makes me think it is symbolic of my insecurities. I am fully clothed but my insecurities are sweeping over me and taking my air like a boa constrictor going in for the kill.

'Well, it is bad. You wouldn't understand.'

'Maybe not but try me. If you want to, that is.'

The bartender arrives and my new friend orders us a round of drinks and insists that I shouldn't refuse. Three mojitos later and he has been given the low down on the Greg, Kate and Kirsty saga. He looks pensive after I stop rambling and I feel a bit silly for pouring it all out.

'I think you are right. It is not good. Lady, I know it seems like this man rescued you from Tom but it sounds to me like he saw you were weak and he pounced. That guy ain't leaving his wife. You mark my words. You go home, you delete his number and you leave him alone. If he wants you like he says he does, he'll pack his bags and come looking for you but if you want my advice, you run away. If he can lie to her like that, he will lie to you like that. I've heard these stories before.

You're his arm candy and nothing more. His wife runs his house and you run his trousers. Nothing more.'

I was about to burst into tears.

'Hey, this isn't your fault. It was an error of judgement perhaps but you can still walk away. Men like this are everywhere and you will never feel better than you do right now if you allow this to continue. If you leave him, I believe that you will feel much better very soon. You can't have a healthy relationship based on how this started. He has low self-esteem and he's dragging you down with him. Let him fuck his own life up, don't let him destroy yours. And one other thing, you won't be his first.'

I knocked back my drink and checked the time. Forty minutes until my cab would be here to take me home.

'My turn to get you a drink and you have forty minutes to tell me about why you are here and send me off feeling chirpier than I do now.'

Randy was Canadian and a retired boat captain. His son lived in the city with his wife and two young children who he was visiting. He told me about the joys of being a grandparent and the even greater joys of staying in a nice hotel and not under their roof. He was charming, wise, interesting and non-judgemental. I enjoyed my short time with him and as my cab pulled up outside the hotel, I was leaving feeling much better than I had before I met him. I kissed him on each cheek and said goodbye and climbed in to the car.

'Make the right choice Kate. Any man would be lucky to have you. Find a man that you are lucky to have too.'

The car pulled away and I began my journey back to England. My head was a mess. I didn't know if I had the strength to leave as I was so desperately hoping that Randy was wrong. All I knew is that I was feeling very different leaving this city as I had when I arrived, I was drained.

Chapter 27

Bags checked in and security done. I have never had the going home blues. I have always felt ready to go home and sleep in my own bed, unpack, do the washing and show off my tan. Going home has never been a problem, until now. Normally, after such a fantastic holiday you would be all over your partner, kissing, cuddling, holding hands, one last splurge in the duty free but not today. After the holiday of a lifetime, I am returning home alone and it's unbearable. I'm not aching to be with him but what's killing me is the incessant overthinking. *Is he a good guy? Is he worth the wait? Will he deliver?* Not only is my internal dialogue torturing me with the constant questions, it is also savvy enough to remind me that if he was what I thought he was or hoping he was I wouldn't be asking these questions in the first place.

I seek refuge in the Irish bar and get myself one more for the road. Who am I kidding? One more that I have to pay for before boarding my flight and taking advantage of the on-board bar. I perch up at a table with two high bar stools and put my earphones in. I am not listening to music or calling anyone, I just don't want to be approached. I am not in the mood to make airport small talk. I take a big sip on my rum and coke before I am disturbed;

'Hello? Hello Kate? Are you there? Hola?' I look around confused, trying to find who is calling my name. 'Hola, Kate? Are you there?'

Suddenly the glare from my phone becomes obvious and I can't believe it took me this long to register it was a call. Crickey, I was more pissed than I realised.

'Um hello? Can you hear me? Sorry the line has been awful. Hello?'

'Kate! It's Maria. Are you still ok to talk?' *Maria? Who the fuck is Maria?*

'Umm yeah ok.'

'Great. I will go and join the guys in the boardroom and we will skype you straight back. Speak in 2 secs.' The phone goes dead. *Skype in 2 secs? Who is she?* I am racking my brains when it suddenly hits me. Maria is from Jones and Lunter LLP! Before I have time to understand how this is happening the skype call comes in. Oh well, what do I have to lose?

Forty-five minutes later we are all laughing, smiling and saying goodbye. I press end call and sip my drink with the completely melted ice in it. I am not sure what happened, I just did the best I could but I think it was fairly obvious I was tipsy. That can't be good.

First things first, I go through my emails to see how this happened and then I find it. I emailed them on my birthday. It would have been around the time Greg was asleep and sunbathing on the hotel roof and I was having my bratty five minutes because he wasn't paying me enough attention. I emailed Maria and we arranged a telephone interview with her, her boss and another company director. Oh well, there will be other companies in Barcelona. I am a big believer in fate. I screwed this up because Greg and I have unfinished business. This is a good thing. This gives me time to sort out us and then plan my life. I just don't feel like I am ready to give up on him yet and if I am honest, I am pissed off that I fucked up that interview. It was the perfect job and part of me holds Greg responsible.

As I finish my drink I glance over at the departure board and see that my flight is boarding. Oddly, I feel better about that than I should. It dawns on me that everything in this relationship is measured. We just have to get to Christmas and he'll leave. I just have to get home and he won't be far behind me. We only have to go five weeks and we will go to Boston together. It's staggered. It's always staggered and its torturous. I just need to board this flight and close my bloody eyes and go to sleep.

Seat belt fastened, bag stowed away. I take my phone out and see that I have received a Whatsapp message. It's Greg. 'I am so sorry you are going home alone. I never knew you would be that upset. I never knew I would cry! That's another thing we have done together now, cry. That should tell you how I feel about us, Kate. It's you and me and I promise you I will make it all worthwhile. We are going to have a fantastic life together. I can't wait to get back and to hold you, kiss you, make love to you. I'm hard now just thinking about it xxxx.' He was doing so well. That last bit told me everything I needed to know.

I replied with nothing more than few kisses. I felt numb. I turned my phone onto Airplane Mode and put it away. Facing away from my stranger neighbours, I look out of the window and begin to cry. Despite not being able to figure out what Greg's intentions are, despite not knowing what to do next, the only thing I can be sure of is that I have never felt like this coming home from a holiday before and I don't want to feel like it ever again. I press my forehead against the window and let the tears stream.

Chapter 28

Dear Greg,

It is with deep regret that I find myself writing you this email, but I must. I cannot talk to you about this face to face because if I am completely honest, I am weak. I will try to tell you how I feel and you will have all the answers as you always do and that will cloud my judgement, as it has done, throughout this.

I need time. This is not the kind of relationship I want and it is hurting me. You seem to be going along with it quite easily and yet, you know it hurts me. I can't keep on going this way. I need some time out. I need to think clearly.

I'm sorry. I know you just took me away on a fantastic trip and it was! It was fantastic but there is always a BUT. The but is that it was a fantastic trip but I spent the last day crying several times and came home feeling utterly lousy. I can't keep doing this to myself.

This all happened at the wrong time. We should've waited until you had moved out. I am not cut out for this kind of sacrifice and that is exactly what it is. A huge sacrifice, probably, on both parts. I'm not sure if the highs are worth the lows anymore.

I'm sorry. I love you BUT I need to think this over.

K xxx

After I had returned home, I spent a couple of days in solitude. Normally I would be desperate to see my friends and tell them the stories. I knew they would see my sadness and that they would all tell me what I already knew so I decided to keep away from them and ask myself, *what did I really want?* Forget what my friends think, forget what Greg wants. I needed to know what I wanted but every time I gave it any thought it hurt. It hurt me that Greg wasn't mine. It hurt me that he didn't seem to care that I was hurting. I wanted a future. I wanted to get married and have children but this relationship didn't seem to be going anywhere.

Greg had already said, that when he eventually moved out that we would have to pretend to his kids that we had only just got together otherwise they would be upset. That alone added another couple of years before we could get married and think about children. He just didn't seem to ever see things from my point of view. Why should I give up on all my dreams for a man that didn't want to see things from my point of view? I couldn't and I wouldn't. I didn't know what hurt more. The idea of breaking up with Greg or the reality that I was actually just a bit of fun to him when he was the love of my life to me.

I sent the email thirty-six hours before he was due to return home. I knew it would have ramifications but I had to be strong. The only way I could get through it would be to ignore my phone for a while. I sent my friends and family a message on Facebook and told them I had broken my phone and that they should contact me on there until I get a replacement. I would turn my phone on when he was back and deal with his response then.

In those thirty-six hours, I blitzed my flat and cleaned it from top to bottom. I had a clear out of my clothes. Something in me had changed and I started to realise that I hadn't been myself for some time. I threw away the clothes that made me look too old and decided that it was about time to have some fun and stop making everything so serious. In my quest to find a husband and life partner I had completely lost myself. Once I had bagged up all the clothes that were dragging me down, I got dressed in my running gear. Running was my escapism, well along with alcohol and the odd cigarette but running was my daytime escapism.

When I came back, sweaty and out of breath, I was disappointed that I had thought about Greg the whole time and I was desperate to know if he had replied to my email. I had gone through various ideas of what his response might be and then I panicked that he might agree that he wants out. I had a sudden urge to tell him I was being an idiot, that I was just being hormonal and that I could wait for him. I would wait for as long as it took.

I checked the time and he would be boarding in twenty minutes. What the hell was I thinking? What if he boarded the flight and something happened. I couldn't leave it like that. I had to tell him I love him. I turned my phone on and the messages came through thick and fast but I didn't stop to read them, there wasn't time. The phone rang;

'Hey baby! I'm so glad you called. Please...'

'No let me. I'm so sorry. I am a selfish bitch. I should never have written that to you before you fly home. I'm sorry. I'm so sorry.'

'Hey. Ssssh. It's ok. I understand why you did. Have you read my replies?'

'No, I just wanted to make sure I spoke to you before you take off. My phone has been off.'

'Ok well when you get off this call, I think you will be pleased. It's you and me baby. I know it's been tough but it is going to be so worth it. I promise. You're my girl. I've waited all my life for someone like you and do you know what else? I love how much you want this too.'

'Oh god I do want it, Greg. I want it so bloody much.'

'Good. Well don't fret. I'm fine, I'll be home soon and I might even have a gift for you. I love you. Have a glass of wine and I will see you tomorrow.'

'I love you too. Please let me know as soon as you land. Bye.'

'Bye.'

It still hurt to hear him say home about a home that isn't our home but I can't keep scrutinising over every detail. I look at my phone and begin checking my messages. Several texts asking me to turn my phone on and him telling me he loves me. Numerous love quotes on Whatsapp and a reply to my email telling me to call him but most surprisingly he had emailed me the details of three properties he had arranged to view when he got back. I let out a sigh of contentment. I felt better. This changed everything. He booked those off his own back which told me he wanted this as much as I did. I was at ease knowing we had fixed the problem and I was not ready to give him up. I would just have to hang in there a little bit longer. Then I saw it. An email from Jones and Lunter LLP.

"Dear Kate,

I have tried to call your number a few times but it doesn't seem to want to connect. Please can you call me?

I wouldn't normally put this in writing but time is ticking along and we need an answer.

We would like to offer you an account management position here in our Barcelona office and need to discuss a start date asap.

Accommodation for the first month is free in our corporate let in the city centre and can be offered at a reduced market price for another month if required.

The salary is fifty-five thousand euros per annum with five percent commission. As expected we will also include a company car, company laptop and company mobile telephone.

We are hoping for as near to an immediate start as possible.

Please call me as soon as you get this.

Maria."

My jaw hit the floor. My dream job in my favourite city and with more money *but* the wrong time. *The wrong fucking time!* I sank my face into my pillow and sobbed.

Later that afternoon I drafted a response to Maria. I couldn't call her. If I did I would take the job because it was exactly what I wanted. Everything happens for a reason. If Greg hadn't have booked those viewings then I would accept the Barcelona job right away but maybe

Barcelona wasn't my destiny. Greg was. I hoped Greg was and I saved my draft to Maria and went and poured some wine.

I woke up the next morning and checked my phone immediately. I was buzzing to see Greg and make up for the email I sent and celebrate the viewings he had booked. I check my texts;

'Hey baby. Landed safe and sound. I'm not going to be able to see you today, or tomorrow. Kirsty has made plans for me to be with the boys and I can't say no having been away for a week. Put me in your diary for the day after and be ready for me. I'll be hungry for you. You sexy minx, you xxxx'

'Aaaaaaahhhhhhh!!!' I punched my pillow furiously. 'This is bullshit.' In a rage, I got up and stormed through to the kitchen and boiled the kettle. Whilst it did that I emailed Maria.

"Dear Maria,

Thank you so much for your email. I gladly accept. Please call when you can to discuss the details.

I'm very excited!

Kind Regards,

Kate"

I left the coffee cup on the side and put on my running gear. I needed to sweat out my emotions.

Chapter 29

I never replied to Greg's text that day and he didn't contact me. Maria called and we went over the details and I said I would speak to my boss about the earliest date in which I could leave. They wanted me yesterday but I had a month's notice to give. Maria suggested that I offer up any commission I was owed as an early release settlement.

A couple of days passed and Greg messaged asking how I was and when could he see me. I felt numb. It seemed to me that we were back on home turf and it was crystal clear that there is no room for me in his life here. Kirsty still tells him what to do. He will never get away from her and even if he did, based on how she has been about him leaving, I would forever be playing second fiddle to her demands. She won't ever let him move on. I can't accept that for me. I have accepted enough. I have tried my best to understand. I have tried to be patient. I have tried to see everything from his point of view and whether he means it or not, this relationship is hurting me. I have to put an end to it.

I reply to his message telling him to meet me in a coffee shop. He replied with 'Ok' and nothing else. He knows what's coming.

As I get ready to meet him I feel like someone has died. I float around the flat as if life has no meaning and I feel pathetic and completely pitiful. I go over and over conversations we have and for every sign that I think I might have missed I remember something he did or said to counteract my disbelief. It was driving me crazy. I couldn't bear the thought of it being over but in truth, it never really began. He was filling me full of false hope. He was stringing me along. Tears pricked my eyes. I pull myself together before the emotion took over and take some deep breaths. *Come on Kate, he's had long enough. He's playing with you.* I inhale deeply once more and leave the house.

Driving along the motorway every song that comes on the radio reminds me of him. I agitatedly flick through the channels repeatedly hoping for something uplifting but there is no getting away from love and heartbreak in music so it seems. Fighting back the overwhelming desire to break down I park the car and head towards the café. I start going over the impending conversation in my head. I need to get it out and get it over with. He will try and take over, he will try and fill my head with more lies and bullshit promises. I need to focus and be strong.

As I open the door in seemingly slow motion, he is facing me. He is early and he has positioned himself at a table that I would see as soon as I walk in. He leaps up out of his seat and rushes towards me, kissing me on my cheek and removing my coat in a mini whirlwind. Next, we are at the counter and he has his arm round my waist and he is ordering my coffee just how I like it and a piece of cake that I wouldn't have opted for but that I apparently deserve and my hips need it, he jokes with the waitress. *He's doing it already. He's taking over the situation trying to prevent what's coming.*

He places his hand on the bottom of my back and guides me towards our table. He nods at the people on the table either side of us and I feel like he is rallying the troops. Instantly he starts talking but I can't hear what he is saying. The cacophony of noise is swirling in my ears and all I can think is that I am about to end this despite being madly in love with him. The truth is, I don't know if the man I am in love with actually exists. I am in love with who he shows me but I fear that he has a different face for every person.

'So, what do you think? Kate? Kate?'

I snap out of my daydream and am drawn to a set of property particulars set out in front of me. 'Sorry, what?'

'Look, I know your mind wandered off but it's ok. Listen now though. I have been viewing properties and this is the one I like. I can see us living there. There is room for me and the kids to begin with and then, when we break the news of our relationship, there is room for you too. See, we will all be together, as I have always promised.'

I look down and then around and then down again. Anywhere but his eyes. I can't meet his eyes or I will crumble.

'The thing is, Greg. It's too late.' My voice begins to whimper and I fight to swallow the lump in my throat.

'Kate don't say that. It's not too late. Don't give up now. I will take the house. I will phone them now and pay the deposit.'

Suddenly questions are spinning around my head furiously and I want the answers. I suppose they have always been there but I have suppressed them.

'Has it only ever been me?'

'What?'

'Since we have been together, has it only ever been me... sexually.'

'What? What sort of question is that?'

'I find it hard to believe that in the time we have been together that you have not had sex with your wife.'

His face flares to a shade of crimson immediately. I push my untouched cake at him and stand up in a hurry.

'Fuck you.' I exit the café before I burst into tears and give the already gloating punters more to look at. I do the quickest walk I can without running and can hear Greg making progress.

'Kate, wait! Kate please.' He grabs my shoulder and pulls me to him. Now I am sobbing.

'Let's talk about this properly. I can explain.'

'You have said enough. I feel sick. How could you, Greg! How fucking could you! You promised me it was over but the whole time... the whole fucking time you were just having your cake and eating it. Well I hope it was worth it. I hope you enjoy seeing me in the world of hell you have catapulted me in to. I never agreed to share you Greg. Not once. Get off me, I'm going home to finish packing.'

'Packing? Where are you going? When do you get back?'

'I've accepted a job in Barcelona. I'm leaving you Greg.' I continue to sob as I turn my back on him and walk away. He was left fixed to the spot also in tears.

By the time I got home I had twelve missed calls, six voicemails and several texts. All of which were from Greg and all telling me how much he loves me and that we need to talk. The last one said he can't go on without me. I rush into my flat, turn my phone off and pour a glass of wine. I pull out my laptop and email my boss. I request a meeting with him in the morning and tell him why.

I feel like I want to throw up. That look on his face. He hadn't kept himself for me. He had been with her meaning that they can't be over? Was it a one-time thing? Had it happened more than once? Did she even know about me? Was this an affair? I slumped down off the couch and rolled onto the floor and screamed into a cushion.

My biggest fear had been confirmed. I was stupid. I was a fucking idiot. He had played me the whole time. Promising me this, promising me that when really, he saw a vulnerable girl breaking up from a toxic relationship and made his swoop. What a sick bastard. I stand up and neck my glass of wine. Looking around the room the rage sets in and I start emptying drawers and pulling down pictures. This was to be a fresh start. I never wanted to see these pictures again or even have these possessions. I needed a clean break. A new job, a new home, a new city, a new country. I needed to get as far the fuck away from him as possible.

The door buzzes and I know it's him but I am keen to see him. I am in full swing of my anger outbreak and I am going to let him have it.

As I open the door he collapses to his knees and wraps his hands around my ankles and is sobbing uncontrollably.

'Get up before my neighbours see you.'

'Kate please! I am begging you. Hear me out.' I kick his hands off my ankles and he stands up. He looks around and then at me. 'What the fuck is going on?'

'I told you. I'm leaving.'

'But... how? What could you have possibly organised in two hours?'

'Well obviously it hasn't been organised in two hours you fucking moron but it's amazing what you can do in two hours, like, fuck your wife? How could you? How could you be with her and not think of me? How could you be with me and not think of her? Did you think anything at all? I feel sick just thinking about it.'

'Kate, it was just once. It was at the beginning. When you and I began. Just one time I promise you. You have to believe me.' Tears are streaming from his swollen eyes and his nose is running down his face. He looks pathetic and only now am I beginning to see who he is.

'Just the once. Just one time. Had we slept together at this point?' He stares at me. 'Answer me then? Had we fucking slept together at this point?' He nods and puts his head in his hands and sobs some more.

'You make me fucking sick. Don't touch me.' I back away from him and look at him again. 'Swear on your children's lives that it was just once.' He looks up at me again and cries. My stomach lurches and I run to the toilet locking the door behind me. I heave several times until it stops and then it's my turn to sob. He's been sleeping with us both. I feel ill. I feel cold. I feel devastated. I feel incredibly stupid. He is wittering on behind the door about how it was only once. Another lie. He tells me over and over again that he loves me and that it's me he wants.

I can't make out everything he says as my mental memory box is playing scenes of our happy times together in my mind and I cannot get over the physical ache in my body. Despite what he says, it doesn't matter what his reasons are or how sorry he is, I could never do what he has done and that tells me that we are not the same. Maybe he does love me, who knows. He probably doesn't know what love is.

I pull myself up off the floor and look at myself in the mirror. I look like I've seen a ghost. Maybe it's because I feel dead inside. I come out of the bathroom and he is slumped on the floor. He tries to take my hand as I walk past him and I tell him again not to touch me.

'Kate, please. I will do anything to make this right. Anything. I am begging you...' Once again, my mind drifts off as he continues to bleat on about his own suffering.

I continue to pack up my belongings into the late hours of the evening with him flitting around next to me, constantly spewing his emotions out completely unaware of how utterly selfish and self-absorbed he is.

It is late and I tell him to leave. He is still talking as I shut the front door on him as he continues to cry.

The next morning I awoke late to several missed calls from Ryan and just as I went to put my phone down another call from him was coming in.

'Morning', I grumbled in a dispirited voice.

'Kate, I will get straight to the point. I need to talk to you about Greg.'

'There is no Greg.'

'What? Actually, let me speak. I know how changeable your romantic mind can be. Kate, there is no easy way for me to tell you this but Greg and Kirsty are not separated. In fact, they are very much together. He has just booked a trip for them to Portugal. Them and a couple they are friends with. No kids, adults only.'

'What? How do you know this?' I was fighting back the tears and desperate to avoid the predestined 'I told you so'.

'Someone I know, knows someone that knows them... it's a long-winded story but Kate, they haven't separated. Kirsty has no idea. He's taking her away on an adult only break. Does that sound like a marriage in crisis to you?'

'Portugal?'

'What?'

'He's taking her to Portugal.' The floodgates opened and the stress of the last few months poured out of me as if a dam became unstuck. The tears poured and poured and I could hardly breathe. I was inconsolable. Ryan came over that evening and I told him everything. Although he didn't want me to go to Barcelona, he agreed that given the circumstances it was the right thing to do.

One week later and I was there. I was in Barcelona. Due to some management changes in our department my boss let me leave right away. It was the blessing I needed. I couldn't handle any more of Greg turning up at the flat unannounced or find him waiting there for me when I got home. It seemed to me that he didn't believe I was really going. It got harder as the days went on and if it wasn't for Barcelona I think I may have crumbled but all I had to do was close my eyes and see him with her and that was enough to make me keep my distance.

The night before my farewell departure I met Ryan at the Coco Loco for some goodbye cocktails. Katya and Gerrard came and Stacey too. A couple of my work colleagues popped in. Everyone seemed more upset about my departure than I had expected despite me reminding them it was only a two-hour flight and that I would be back to visit but most of them wanted to come and visit me, not surprising really. Despite the sadness the general consensus was there, I must get away from Greg. When the day came, I gave him the wrong airport and flight details in case he made one last attempt to stop me.

I slept on the flight on the way over completely drained and fearful about what I had left behind and what was ahead for me. Knowing that I would not have to see Greg on a daily basis reassured me that I would get over this in time. I felt so stupid. Stupid, naïve and blind. It had all become clear once it had been spelt out to me. It was glaringly obvious they hadn't split but I didn't see it or maybe I didn't want to see it. He promised to rescue me from Tom and I believed him. I didn't think he wanted to abuse me when I was escaping abuse. That hurt. In fact, it fucking hurt. I was devastated. I wanted to believe he loved me and wanted to be with me. How could I have got it so wrong? If I had stayed, I don't know if I would have had the strength to leave. Stupidly, I was still in love with him. I don't know why, perhaps because he was never really mine.

As I unpack in my temporary accommodation, I can't help but feel excited about my new beginning. Maria met me at the airport and talked enthusiastically all the way in the taxi to the house. She was very cool and oozed Mediterranean chic style. Long flowing dark hair, olive skin and curves in all the right places. She tells me to get ready and that we are going out in an hour for dinner and to meet some of my new colleagues. I feel good. I feel excited. New beginnings and new memories ahead for me.

We meet some of the others at a restaurant in Colon Square. Although it's late autumn it's still warm enough to sit outside. One of the many reasons I love being abroad and now I get to call it home. I feel happy and peaceful. I hadn't been at peace in months.

Everyone is really friendly and the conversation is as plentiful as the bread and dipping oil being passed around and the wine consumed. No doubt I won't remember who's who in the morning but I have time to get to know my new colleagues. There was a German guy, an Italian girl and several Spaniards. All of them were young, hip and full of life and all promised to take me under their wing and show me the Catalonian way of life.

Eventually we decide to call it a night and Maria says she will come back with me and stay at the staff house so that I don't get lost. She's very easy to get along with and we laugh and giggle like two schoolgirls. It feels like it has been a long time since I have laughed and felt this carefree. I'm very glad she is escorting me home. I need to keep as busy and as distracted as possible.

As I lay my head on my freshly laundered pillow, I am grinning from ear to ear. Life is good and I will be ok. This was absolutely the right thing to do.

'Knock knock. Sorry to disturb you Kate but you don't have a spare tampon do you? I left mine back at my apartment.'

'Yeah sure.' I scramble out of bed, turn the light on and start rummaging through my toiletries. 'Aha! Here we go. Take your pick.' Maria takes one and apologises again.

Once back in bed and minutes before dozing off something hits me like a brick. I'm late. I haven't had a period in about six weeks. I begin to panic and scramble around for my phone. I quickly open the calendar app and start scrolling through the dates.

'Fuck. Fuckety fuck fuck. It can't be.' I sit upright and rub my temples. I jolt out of bed and go back to the toiletries box. I'm pretty certain I have an emergency pregnancy kit in there. Once retrieved, nimbly I make my way to the shared bathroom praying not to wake anyone. Inside with the door locked, I pace up and down looking at the plastic stick and biting my lip. *It's got to be stress. They say stress can make you late. That will be it.* Frantically I peel off the wrapper and do the deed. It says it needs two minutes. I put it face down next to the toothbrush holder whilst I wash my hands. My mind is racing. *It can't be. We were careful. I would've known if we'd had an accident.*

I pick up the tiny stick with trembling hands. This could be life changing but then again, and more likely, it could be nothing and I'm just late. All women have scares. That's why we all have emergency pregnancy kits. I'm worrying. I'm panicking. Reading the box one more time, one line for not pregnant and two lines means pregnant. I grab the stick, take a deep breath and turn it over.

'Oh, baby.'

About the Author

Lucinda is 31 years old in lives in Hampshire. Born in Aberdeenshire, she spent the early years of her life in a small fishing town before relocating with her mother to the South Coast.

She is the middle child and only girl with four brothers.

Lucinda began her higher education in studying Performing Arts and then began a degree in Law (but dropped out). She is a qualified hairdresser but the arts always drew her back in and she took up an interest in writing which she now plans to continue to make a career out of.

Mother of one, a baby boy, she works part time for a Business publication and spends her spare time soaking up the Hampshire countryside and plotting her next stories.

Printed in Great Britain
by Amazon